Contemporary Christianity
in Arunachal Pradesh
Intra-Extra Conversion Issues

Contemporary Christianity in Arunachal Pradesh Intra-Extra Conversion Issues

Tado Lishi

2019

Contemporary Christianity in Arunachal Pradesh: Intra-Extra Conversion Issues - published by the Rev. Dr. Ashish Amos of the Indian Society for Promoting Christian Knowledge (ISPCK), Post Box 1585, Kashmere Gate, Delhi-110006.

© Author, 2019

ISBN: 978-93-88945-23-3

Laser typeset by

ISPCK, Post Box 1585, 1654, Madarsa Road, Kashmere Gate, Delhi-110006 • *Tel:* 23866323

e-mail: ashish@ispck.org.in • ella@ispck.org.in
website: www.ispck.org.in

Contents

Acknowledgments

At the outset, I thank Almighty God, whose abundant grace in Christ Jesus has enabled me to write this book. I am thankful to my principal resourceful person, Professor Allan H. Anderson, whose patience and invaluable guidance has immensely been encouraging me to accomplish this study.

This first, and incredibly significant, study on the contemporary Christianity in the remotest part of Northeast India would have not been possible without the open-hearted participation and co-operation of the leaders and members of the Christian Revival Church, Itanagar, Arunachal Pradesh. My most sincere thanks go to Pastor Tap Taluk and Evangelist Brother Joram Dol who humanely helped in distributing my survey and collecting the responses from the church members. Significantly, I thank and highly appreciate all the leaders and members who participated in this research. I also express my gratitude to some other denominations Church leaders and members for their assist in contributing to my findings on the development of Christian unity in the state, through informal interactions.

I am forever thankful for the constant love, support, and encouragement of my loving and self-confident wife, Yaya Lishi, and my three humorous children, Akin, Anya and Hoboku Lishi, who have sustained me so well throughout my studies in the United Kingdom.

Finally, I extremely thankful to ISPCK for considering my request of publishing this book through their publication. Especially, I am heartily thankful to Rev. Dr. Ashish Amos of the Indian Society for Promoting Christian Knowledge for finalising this work as book form.

Foreword

Mr. Tado Lishi has been an enthusiastic researcher and theological educator who have contributed well in the field of theological education in the region of Arunachal Pradesh. When I first met him here in Bangalore at United Theological College, a decade ago, he was a soft speaker, but with passionate Bachelor of Divinity student. Later he became the Principal of a Bible seminary in Arunachal Pradesh that inspired him to move to United Kingdom for his master's studies.

After the successful completion of his research study, he returned to India to take up various responsibilities in the church under the banner of Nyishi Baptist Church Council, Arunachal Pradesh, India.

In India, the ministry of publication should be taken up by many people in order to provide theological foundation for the ecclesial debates, especially, in the region from where this young scholar is rising up, where the church is comparatively young, many should willingly shoulder the task, the one which this young scholar has initiated. This book is an outcome of the author's hard works, systematic and rigorous study in the field of theology, both nationally and abroad.

I do hope and pray that the publication of this book will enrich the Christian literature well in the region. The Christian literature in the region will have a new phase with this contribution from a younger scholar. I am sure; this work will be received very well, as many readers will benefit from this study.

C. I. David Joy

Professor, UTC, Bangalore

Chapter 1
Arunachal Pradesh at a Glance

Although this book is not primarily concerned with the history of Arunachal Pradesh, it is important to begin this book with a glance of Arunachal Pradesh since this book is one of the first books on contemporary Christianity in the region. The book focuses on Christian religious conversion and adaptation, related movements, changing religious scenario, the spiritual and doctrinal confusion within Christianity that emerged from the Pentecostal-Charismatic based structure of church in the state. It would indeed, be helpful for readers especially from outside Arunachal Pradesh.

Arunachal Pradesh, formerly known as the North-East Frontier Agency (NEFA), is still known to be the area with the longest disputed border between China and India since antiquity. History informs us that the arrival of the British administration in the Assam region, sometime in the late 18th century, brought about assured resolution to the long-standing border dispute.[1] Present-day Arunachal Pradesh covers a physical area of 83,743 Sq. km, which is roughly 2.55% of the total area of the whole of India, and lies between the latitudes 26030' north and longitudes 91030' east. Forming India's international frontier with China and Tibet along the snow-clad mountains of the extreme north, its territory extends its meeting point with Bhutan to the west about 1,030 km., then moving east, and then linking it to the southeast, Arunachal Pradesh forms the border with Myanmar for about 441km.[2]

People and Languages

Arunachal Pradesh is home to numerous ethnic groups, mostly of Asiatic derivation who are in some ways linked to the Tibetans and the ethnic minority groups of the hills of Myanmar. Roughly two-thirds of the province's denizens are formally labelled as 'Scheduled Tribes' (an appellation that commonly relates to indigenous peoples), who are considered to be somehow outside of the predominant Indian social structure.[3] The Nyishi, who constitute the largest ethnic group of the state, along with the Sherdukpen, Aka, Monpa, Apatani, and Hill Miri peoples, inhabit western Arunachal. The Adi, who are second in number to the Nyishi in Arunachal Pradesh, live predominantly in the central area of the state. In the north-eastern hill area lives a small ethnic group called the Mishmi. The Wancho, Nocte and Tangsa peoples occupy the south-east. There are 50 spoken dialects in the state, mostly related to the Tibeto-Myanmar linguistic group. Barriers between many dialects necessitated Assamese and Hindi, the two Indo-Aryan languages, and also English, to be used as common languages in the region. Each tribe has its own social, cultural, and beliefs stems, and are generally endogamous (marrying within the group).

Socio-Economic Life

Until two to three decades' past, the economic system of Arunachal Pradesh was totally independent of the village community life. Natural and organic resources were the main economies of the people through agriculture cultivation. These were always considered as the instant raw or cooked food for daily life those were available most of the season, except during the extreme winter season. The value of physical works counted as the product of good cultivation. As Pandey reiterates, "Till the recent times, the economic activities of the people of Arunachal Pradesh continued to be a large subsistence nature based on agriculture."[4] In relations to major economic resources, the cattle like mithun, cows, goats, pigs and chicken were reared and tamed within the locality.[5] However, in recent decades, the economic system of the state has significantly improved in many ways, through the agricultural projects initiated by the government of India after the declaration of an independent state in 1978, by the then Prime Minister of India late Indira Gandhi.

Socio-Religious Life

The religious system of Arunachal Pradesh has, historically, always been variegated, and one can identify that there have been times, when there was no proper religion, except the indigenous belief systems worshipped and paid homage to the natural world. Tako Davi identifies that, overall, European writers often held the view that ethnic groups of the state did not have any 'proper' religion or religious system. Animism' was considered to be the best term to describe the belief system of these people.[6] Following the historical belief of Buddhism in Arunachal, is considered Buddhism as the state religion, which is mainly followed by the Monpas people residing in Tawang district in the east, close to Bhutan, which is predominantly Mahayana Buddhist.[7]

In the early 20th century, a new religion called Donyi-Poloism (DP) was founded and propagated in the region.[8] Donyi-Poloism is considered to be a counter-religious movement in response to the emergence of Christianity.[9] It is founded on the traditional oral beliefs of the ancestors who, through physical observances, believed the Sun to be the mother and the Moon as the father of humanity – the life giver and the life keeper, respectively.[10] According to Bani Danggen, Donyi-Poloism has been followed only by the Adi, which is the second largest ethnic group in the region, (and are also known to be the most literate ethnic group in AP).[11] In late 20th century some British anthropologists, such as E. T. Dalton, G. D. S. Dunbar, and V. Elwin,[12] visited some of the rural areas inhabited by the Adi and identified significant number of supernatural phenomena which Adi termed as the 'spirit of the demon.' However, contemporary Donyi-Polo literature refuted this term as a misinterpretation of ethnic minority belief systems, thereby invalidating the findings of those British anthropologists as misguided one.[13]

Talom Rikbo,[14] who is known to be the founder of the modern Donyi-Polo movement, professes that, as humans ultimately receive all energy source from the Sun, Donyi-Polo should truly be worshipped as reflected upon the supreme being of the unseen supernatural God in the form of the Sun and the Moon.[15] However, through a careful observation of Talom Rikbo's teachings on the faith, doctrine, and dogmas of Donyi-Polo, the movement can indirectly be seen as replicating Christian faith and practices.[16]

Regarding the arrival of Christianity in Arunachal Pradesh, it is somewhat difficult to accurately trace its history authentically, owing to the lack of proper written records, even though it is a fast-growing mission. The indirect historical record states that although Christianity has already been in the hills area before the British Administration reached in the late 18th or early 19th century, however, was not properly introduced. Liankhankhup explains that, "the history of Christianity in Arunachal Pradesh has been traced as early as the arrival of Mrs. C.A Bruce in 1834 and Rev. Nathan Brown, the first American Baptist Missionary to reach Sadiya on March 23, 1836."[17] Jagdish Lal Dawar argues that although Christianity reached Arunachal in the early nineteenth century, it was not considered to be a successful mission until the late nineteenth century, when native people accepted the Christian faith and initiated mission work.[18] Accordingly to some elders in the region, the 1960's and 70's were the peak decades of Christian growth in Arunachal Pradesh, which was followed by severe persecution of the indigenous people, which was implicitly or explicitly sanctioned by Hindu nationalists in the Government systems.[19]

Despite the fast growth of mainline Christianity in the region, with its significant mission plans and strategies for progression, there are also certain areas of perplexity within Christianity in the region, owing to denominationalism and issues of intra-proselytisation.[20] One example of misperception is a method of easy shifting of faith groups within Christianity. Specifically, this is prevalent in the conversion strategy of the Christian Revival Church movement. The flexible method of conversion/change within Christianity has been identified as a problem not only within Christianity but with other faiths as well.[21] For instance, the Indigenous Faith and Cultural Society of Arunachal Pradesh identify Charismatic Christianity as a wavering and ever-shifting faith practice in the region.[22] Those who adhere to indigenous religions and other faiths often criticise the changing mission methods of Christianity, considering them to be a real threat to the cultural integration of the frontier Tribal people. In particular, Charismatic Christians' exhibition of holy and unholy show insolence towards other faiths or within the Christian churches. Charismatic Christianity's dominating influence upon other faiths have caused difficulties and practically making Christian theological understanding of conversion/change as conflicting situations.[23]

Interesting developments within the mainline churches, predominantly among the Catholics and Baptists, have recently been the initiation of a movement called the 'Revival Crusade' which aims to maintain church membership.[24] This has come about because, the established churches have realised that the apparent spiritual awakening within the Charismatic churches in the region have ostensibly influenced almost every ethnic groups, in one way or another. Contrarily, the elites within the established churches consider this new 'Revival Crusade' as replicating, what they consider to be this 'immature' religious movement of Charismatic Christianity. Apart from missiological issues, there is also some doctrinal inconsistency, primarily, the misconceptions of spirit and water baptism. The process of conversion/change in Arunachal Pradesh has ominously identified as perplexity, instead of clear Christian mission.[25] Therefore, there is an urgent need for some mediation within Christianity in the region for furtherance of better mission work in the state.

This book attempts to answer the following questions: Why do Charismatic Christian churches consider their movement to be a spiritual crusade? What is the primary force that caused the movement to be so significant within Christianity? And what is the impact on the individual and the family after conversion/change to Christianity and Charismatic Christianity in general and Christian Revival Church in particular through different aspects of movements for change? The key case study congregation, known as Christian Revival Church, is a church located in Itanagar (the capital city of AP), and can be considered to be the largest among Christian Revival Church in the region. The primary reason for concentrating as basis of this book on the Charismatic movement is that significant talks about, and criticisms of, Christian Revival Church and its practices were being spotlighted both from the mainline churches and other faith groups. The religious elites of the region have frequently suggested that Charismatic Christianity is superficial and that the movement is disorganised. As Dawar identifies that converts were alleged to be the harbingers of disharmony and that, "their attitude smacked of arrogance and superiority complex vis-à-vis the non-converts."[26] Sometimes, in some places, speaking in tongues is reportedly misinterpreted, and indeed, there is a phenomenon of glossolalia that has even become a competitive practice within the movement. Apart from the baptism of the spirit, there is a strange practice to the doctrine of baptism called the second water baptism.[27] The practice which relates to the findings of Klaver and Kamp, who identified that, "converts who shifted from mainline churches to Evangelical/Pentecostal churches experience conflicts over the timing and modes of baptism. This shows how different modes of baptism and conversion/change are embedded in distinct forms of embodiment."[28] Michael Bergunder identifies similar issues about water baptism among Pentecostals in southern India.[29] However, these practices are not as strange as the extreme practices of Christian Revival Church in the region which are doctrinally inconsistent. Apart from these internal doctrinal issues there are also some aspects of social efforts initiated by the charismatic movement, especially the Christian Revival Church, which seemed to have considered any sort of transformation as the powerful work of the Holy Spirit, rather than human effort.

Endnotes

[1] Lamb, Alastair, 1964. *The China-India Border: The Origins of the Disputed Boundaries,* London: Oxford University Press, 175-6.

[2] Pandey, Deepak, 2006. *History of Arunachal Pradesh: earliest time to 1972 A.D,* Pasighat: Bani Mandir Publication, 1.

[3] Deryck, Lodrick O. *Arunachal Pradesh State, India,* www.britannica.com/place/Arunachal-Pradesh. Accessed 05.10.2015.

[4] Pandey, *History of Arunachal Pradesh,* 160.

[5] Pandey, *History of Arunachal Pradesh,* 156.

[6] See Davi, Tako, 2004. 'Relevance of Tribal Religion: An Overview' *Understanding Tribal Religion,* (Ed. Tamo, Mibang & Sarit, Chaudhuri K.), New Delhi: Mittal Publications, 9-10.

[7] Drema, Tsering, 'Sacred Places of Monpas of Arunachal Pradesh' *Understanding Tribal Religion,* 210.

[8] *Donyi-Poloism* is the belief in the Sun and Moon as twin deities, from which every source of energy and light comes and sustains all humanity.

[9] Donyi-Poloism is believed to a recent founded religion to backslash Christianity for cultural restoration.

[10] Borang, Kaaling, 2004. 'Philosophy of Donyi-Polo' *Understanding Tribal Religion,* 40-14.

[11] The researcher practically known, the Adi tribe was known as the largest ethnic group in Arunachal Pradesh till 2006. But, in the year 2007 the tribe has been divided into two ethnic groups known as 'Adi and Galo'. However, Adi have the highest numbers of government officers and employees in the state.

[12] Davi, Tako, 2004. 'Relevance of Tribal Religion: An Overview' *Understanding Tribal,* 15.

[13] Danggen, Bani, 2007. *A Comparative Study of Bon Religion of Ancient Tibet with Donyi-Polo Faith of the Adis of Arunachal Pradesh,* Itanagar: Preety Publishers & Distributors, 4-5.

[14] It is reported that Talom Rikbo was a Catholic Christian, and that at one point he had travelled to Italy for theological training. After two years of theological training, he returned to Arunachal Pradesh and founded the modern Donyi-Poloism faith in early 1970.

[15] Rikbo, Talom, 1998. 'Donyi-Polo Faith and Practice of the Adis' in *Indigenous Faith and Practices of the Tribes of Arunachal Pradesh*, (Ed. Behera, M. C. & Chaudhuri, S. K.), Itanagar: Himalaya Publishers, 57-59.

[16] As an example, the Donyi-Poloism uses Christian hymnals, replacing the nouns of 'the Sun' and 'the Moon' in place of God or Jesus.

[17] Liankhankhup, Sektak, *A Study of Hindu and Christian Mission in Arunachal Pradesh/* www.facebook.com/notes/liankhankhup-sektak, accessed on 15.10.2015. This main resource book is only available in the state of Manipur from where the post on Facebook was authenticated, but where I was unable to visit during my fieldwork in December 2015.

[18] Dawar, Jagdish L. 'Religious Conversion and Contending Responses' *Understanding Tribal Religion*, 159-60.

[19] There are some elders in my native village who witnessed the persecutions during the 1970s and 1980s and who narrated their stories to me. The concept of Hindu nationalism is a common one in academia.

[20] The proselytization of Pentecostal-Charismatic Churches from other Church members are considered as the spiritual renewal movement. So they mostly target not to the non-Christian for conversion, but having strategy converting from within the established Church.

[21] This method attempts to convert people from other Church denominations, such as Baptism and Catholicism, along the non-Christian mission strategies and conversion programmes.

[22] The Indigenous Faith and Cultural Society is an organisation formed by the largest ethnic group of the State (Nyishi tribe) who in each and every discussion the preservation of tradition and culture of the frontier state, and term Christianity as a threat to every traditional system. Although they don't have authentic literature, but they are strongly slogan against Christianity in the region.

[23] Dawar, 'Religious Conversion' *Understanding Tribal Religion*, 161.

[24] These days, fasting and prayer programmes in churches and revival crusade conferences are commonly taking place among the mainline churches in order to prevent their members from turning to the CRC crusades and revival camps.

[25] Indigenous Faith and Cultural Society of Arunachal *Pradesh* (IFCSAP) is one of the strongest elite organisations that deals with all sort of religious, cultural and social issues in the state and is formed unanimously by all religious groups.

[26] Dawar, *Understanding Tribal Religion*, 2.

[27] In 2012 one of my relatives who is a Baptist believer faced a serious family problem. He and his wife went to one of the Prayer Centre of CRC. Both wife and husband were asked to re-baptised in order to get some help of counselling for their crisis. They were assured to receive the Baptism of the Holy Spirit followed by the water re-baptism. However, they did not go for it.

[28] Miranda Klaver & Linda van de Kamp, 2011. 'Embodied Temporalities in Global Pentecostal Conversion', *Ethnos*, 76:4, 421-425, DOI: 10.1080/00141844.2011.632691, 423.

[29] Bergunder, Michael, 2008. *The South Indian Pentecostal Movement in the Twentieth Century*, Michigan/Cambridge, Grand Rapids, 236.

Chapter 2

Conversion / Changing Scenario of Religious System

Introduction

This chapter aims to look at different scholars' understandings of the meaning of religious conversion in general, and conversion to Pentecostal-Charismatic Christianity in particular. From practical, historical and theological observations it would seem that not all converts to Pentecostal-Charismatic Christianity can be considered as 'true converts.'[1] This significant observation could be the result of doctrinal, theological and pneumatological confusion, evident within Pentecostal-Charismatic movements, in which views and understanding differs between churches and denominations.[2] This chapter includes the areas of identifying true converts, cause and contributing factors, active and passive after conversion and concludes by looking at the stage model of conversion, outlined by Rambo and other conversion experts.

The Meaning of Conversion/Change

In the Oxford English Dictionary, the term 'conversion' has different meanings depending on its inference and context. There are at least six different contexts identified in the Oxford dictionary in which the word 'conversion' is used: for example, religion, theology, logic, law, biology and sports. Although the meaning of the word differs slightly depending on the context, all relate to the process of changing, or causing something to change from one form to another. In considering the meaning of religious conversion, the theological meaning, simply refers to repentance and a change to a godly life.[3] This theological meaning of change seems to be present practically throughout the history of Christianity, and which can be currently observed all over the world, as Starbuck succinctly notes:

> Throughout Christianity, down to the modern 'revival meeting,' a phenomenon has been prominent, commonly called' conversion. In the Greek, Roman Catholic, Lutheran, Anglican, Episcopal and some other churches, it has a correspondence in confirmation. It is characterised by more or less sudden changes of character from evil to goodness, from sinfulness to righteousness, and from indifference to spiritual insight and activity.[4]

Make a significant change to one's identity always occurs due to some specific reason, including those related to religious and social related issues. Whether it is due to a socio-religious, socio-economic or socio-political factor, when a change such as a conversion occurs, there will certainly have been motives behind it. Social science studies of religion is used as backup source for this study on religious conversion to incorporate the social transformation brought by Christian Revival Church in Arunachal Pradesh. It is necessary to begin with first, the relationship between two religious conversions and the sociology of religion.

Lofland and Skonovd's (1981) study on the typological occurrence of religious conversion represent five types of motifs which encompass the three variations of human life and its relation to social issues: "intellectual, physical, and emotional."[5] These three typologies have been considered by Peter Halama in his study of conversion, and he assesses, in their typology use the term conversion motif to describe a specific process by which conversion occurs. They [Lofland and Skonovd] describe five dimensions of this process: degree of social pressure, a temporal duration, the level of affective arousal, affective content, and belief-behaviour sequence of change.[6]

The reasons behind an attempt to change, according to sociological studies, have frequently been identified as of challenges or issues in the life of an individual which have compelled that person to act upon the context or situation at stake, may it be a social, religious, and political issue.

According to Thomas O'Dea F. in the phase of change occurs, due to the different social stratification caused through people's different attitude toward the situation of the society. The inhabitant's different attitude and exhibitions lead to demand the context for a social and cultural change. These are the factors that also led sociological studies to deal with the issues of religious conversion in society. No society simply depends on the social structure, but it should be seen that religion is present in every social issue.[7] Both intra and extra-Christian conversion occurs due to certain reasons, which may be psychological, economic, political, religious, and also due to certain conflict. The converts also have emotionally connected to the social reasons which compelled converts to make that change of religious beliefs. Regarding intra-Christian converts in the context of Arunachal Pradesh, there are also certain reasons why an individual and a family may decide to change their faith from one group to another. As Robert Orsi argues, "people appropriate religious idioms as they need them, in response to particular circumstances. All religious ideas and impulses are of the moment, invented, taken, borrowed, and improvised at the intersections of life."[8] As Orsi have analysed through sociologists, for example, Max Weber, Emile Durkheim and others, who addressed the social issues in their time and, significantly, identified that conversion to Christianity was often a challenge of social dissatisfaction within the context they lived.[9] While identifying the historical impact of religious conversion in the society, which was significantly studied by Emile Durkheim and Max Weber, Thomas O'Dea argues:

> In our consideration, above of Weber and Durkheim, three things become quite clear. First, inclination toward certain kinds of religious doctrines on the part of people has highly influenced by their social position in society. Secondly, some religious ideas reflect universal characteristics of the human condition and therefore have a wide appeal which transcends the divisions of social stratification. Thirdly, social changes and especially social disorganisation result in a loss of cultural consensus and group solidarity and set men upon a 'quest for community' – that is looking for new values to which they might adhere and new groups to which they might belong. It implies that conversion – the acceptance of new religions – is itself closely related to needs and aspirations which are highly affected by the social circumstances of the involved, although social conditions are not a simple and unique causal element in such cases.[10]

It is obviously reasonable within the strata of every society there has constantly been a certain affiliation between conversion events and the evident social stratification. Without social issues in the society or among the faith groups, the changing from one group to another should not erroneously occur in a particular context.[11] This is clearly discernible in the context of Charismatic movement in the region, which has the challenging factor for elite religious groups of the state, as they observe. The conversion to Christianity could be seen like a variety of ocean waves that suddenly occurs during a storm that washes away everything on the seashore. Conversion, therefore, not only impacts the religious practices of an individual, but also the society, culture, and even politics. In this way, conversion events create further complexity in the context in which they occur.[12] Brusco (1986) points out in her study of Colombian Pentecostalism that Pentecostal social practice and norms inverted the masculine role, making men more accommodating to domestic ideals as opposed to the traditional 'machismo' type of gendered identity. Others have also pointed out that Pentecostal social practice has enabled women to voice their domestic problems.[13] This also entails that gender issues are addressed in the leadership of the Charismatic movement, and indeed, as far as Arunachal Pradesh is concerned, we see that the sharing of leadership is equally engaged among the genders.[14]

Historically, the general understanding of conversion in Christianity appears to have varied from century to century, from time to time, and from place to place. Definitions have therefore been somewhat ambiguous. As Darrol Bryant rightly identifies, conversion meant, "in some contexts, a spiritual process turning one's life to God in Jesus Christ and, in others, a formal confession of the Christian faith and participation in the sacramental life of the Christian Church."[15] Simultaneously, Jeffrey D. Marlette argues that, "converts have been regarded as among the most colourful figures in the history of Christianity; anyone endeavouring to understand them and the period in which they converted faces a treacherous path."[16] Halama asserts that, "there is agreement that no standard way of conversion exists and that there are significant differences in the ways that people convert. There have appeared several typologies of religious conversion with different types or number of types."[17] Halama's analysis of conversion is very comprehensive and complements both Rambo's stage models method and Gooren's notion of the 'conversion career'. However, Rambo's model can be considered to be the most cooperative in understanding any conversion event.

Without a doubt, the exceptional global success of Pentecostal-Charismatic Christianity is owing to its clear focus on evangelism and conversion. To the Pentecostal-Charismatic Christian, if one wishes to come to Christ one must go through certain steps, including immediate conversion. Without this, it is thought, there is no value in becoming a member of the great family of God.

The literature of Lewis L. Rambo on religious conversion is most impressive and can be seen as one of the broadest attempts on this subject. Rambo, writes that, "as I read more deeply in sociological literature, its limitations also became apparent when I began to consider the importance of cultural issues."[18] Rambo's, *Understanding Religious Conversion* is not only the single most comprehensive and compendium collection of the literature on conversion, but it strengthens our understanding of the process of religious conversion and clarifies its meaning. Rambo explains the meaning of religious conversion quite precisely using a clear-cut and solid approach as he writes:

> It will mean simply change from the absence of a faith system to a faith commitment, from religious affiliation with one faith system to another, or from one orientation system to another within a single faith system…a change of one's personal orientation toward life, from the haphazard of superstition…a radical shifting of gears that can take the

spiritually lackadaisical to a new level of intensive concern, commitment, and involvement.[19]

Rambo's definition then makes it comparatively clear what is meant by religious conversion both in terms of intra-religious and extra-religious conversion. Here it is identifiable that, once a person has to change from one faith to another, then that individual should be determined to follow what they have decided, and they should commit to following that path. Rambo's explanation on the true meaning of conversion relates to the context of this research is concerned, in addition to supporting the process of critical analysis and examining the intra-Christian conversions in the region.[20] Concurrently, Walter Conn's understanding on intra-religious conversion poses a crucial question about the social concern of Arunachal Pradesh, which is a significant matter to be solved. Intra-religious conversion within Christianity should be discussed broadly among scholars of conversion, who should find some solutions to these issues. As Conn argues, "conversion from one Christian Church to another has been questioned as the goal of a church's missionary enterprise in an ecumenical age. But these conversions obviously continue, as do the conversions of non-Christians to Christianity."[21]

Appraised by Rambo himself, another contemporary text, which should be prerequisite reading for all students of conversion, is *Religious Conversion and Disaffiliation: Tracing Patterns of Change in Faith Practice* by Henri, Gooren. This helps one comprehensively comprehend not only the meaning of conversion but also contemporary religious issues that relate to conversion. According to Gooren, "conversion is a comprehensive personal change of religious worldview and identity, based on both self-rapport and attribution by other."[22] Gooren's concept of the 'conversion career' classifies the fluctuation system of today's global Christianity. By determining the original New Testament Greek meaning of the word 'conversion' (*metamelomai*), Gooren connects the true lexicon of Christian meaning of conversion, and in doing so, his definition of conversion can be seen as concisely related to the Pentecostal-Charismatic practice of conversion, which is to "turn in a different direction, a turning to and a turning from...a change of mind and a change of heart...and change in identity."[23] Gooren's definition of conversion career adds to a wider understanding of contemporary religious conversion around the world. He understands religious conversion as an ever-changing phenomenon, shifting within different times and space, and occurring throughout the history of humanity along different religious contours, depending on the individual and societal context. One can see Gooren's delineation of conversion careers as "the member's passage, within his or her social and cultural context, through levels, types, and phases of church participation,"[24] as supporting Rambo's meaning and stage models of conversion. It is in fact true that within one individual, different stages of conversion can be identified over time, sometimes within the same wider religious groups and sometimes being stirred to change from one religion to another.

Stage Model in Conversion (Rambo)

Numerous scholars and theologians have attempted to contribute many literature reviews on religious conversion/ change in general understanding with a wide range of meanings and contexts of the subject. On the one hand, students of conversion can use a wealth of scholarly writings on the subject of religious conversion from different disciplines, such as history, theology, sociology, psychology and anthropology. On the other hand, as identified by Kahn and Greene, Rambo's broad multi-dimensional definition of conversion, with its empirically-grounded seven stage model, can be seen to cover other scholars' interpretations of the subject. As Peter remarks, "in so doing, Rambo, both clarifies and limits the boundaries of conversion as adherence to, or defection from, some organised religious body."[25] Although Rambo argues that the seven stages in his model of the conversion process are the points of change, he also clarifies that conversion does not centre on any particular stage. However, according to the cultural setting and context, the conversion process begins naturally.[26] In chapter two and three of *Understanding Religious Conversion*, Rambo methodically outlines how conversion can start from any point within the seven stage models; however, one can perceive social and socio-psychological related issues as being the epicentre of religious conversion, which can be seen as being the case in the context of Arunachal Pradesh.[27]

Following outlined and synthesised theories on religious conversion by Rambo and other conversion scholars, I now move on to delineate the seven stage models, according to Rambo's classification, highlighting how they interlink from one to another.

Context

The meaning and terminology of the word context has no national or ethnic barrier: context affects all things in every human society and community, irrespective of race, religion and colour. Context is the dominant term in every discussion and interaction, whether with regards to religion, politics, and or economics. Without understanding the context of a particular place or people, one cannot develop accurate understandings about them. Therefore, Rambo's use of context as first stage in his model of religious conversion signifies the importance of its powerful influence in human society, including as a catalyst for religious conversion/changing.

Context in Arunachal Pradesh is diverse and in multi-factors which no scholars can easily classify concisely, as it occurs according to the tribal ethnic groups religious practices from place-to-place and community-to-community. The modern contexts in this region seemed to have made more complicated which apparently have led the state in fast changing religious developments in diverse forms. In such varied contexts, there is definitely and reasonably crisis, quest, encounter, interaction, commitment, and consequences have occurred.

Crisis

In a time of an intensely difficult situation; to make a decision is often a turning point for a person/family. This turning point, which could lead one to a serious, decisive situation in one's life journey, is called a crisis in an individual or a household. In such a situation, a psychologist would advise the individual or family, with the help of extensive psychological knowledge. The psychological literature has focused extensively on the notion of crisis as the precipitant to conversion. Likewise, other branches of religious study would assimilate their analysis of conversion, to understand the situation that could have affected the potential converts into changing their mind, depending on the context.[28] As Milton, while analysing Rambo's crisis intensification points out, "the two important issues relating to the crisis stage are 'contextual issues' and 'the degree of activity or passivity of the convert."[29] These will greatly influence the shape and impact of the crisis.[30] Rambo sees the nature of crisis as varied and the process to change could take in two different contexts: the Christian context and the context of other religions, depending upon the socio-cultural situation at stake.

Quest

When a crisis arises in one's life or family, there certainly will follow a point of inquiry: what should one do in such situation? The person in crisis would consider from where and from whom they might be able to receive help and support in finding a solution to their problem. Support given should be able to direct that person or family in having an important effective manner to helping them to change their situation satisfactorily and in an appropriate way, so that the point of change may not later cause regret. This may be the point of changing the whole situations including faith and belief. As Kahn and Greene identify, "the quest motif highlights the potential conversion as actively seeking something 'more' in religious life."[31] Rambo clarifies that 'quest' in life is inevitable, as long as an individual or family exists in the world, "quest is an ongoing process, but one that will greatly intensify during the time of crisis.[32] While Grace Milton views that a solution to a crisis based quest may not necessarily be a religious or spiritual one, and that helping the seeker find an answer from different sources is most important.[33] Milton expresses according to the secular understanding of meeting one's quest in life. However, in the contexts of tribal people, one can precisely observe the religious help and supports during the quest seemed to have the most effective and quickest basis for finding a solution to the situations going through with the solution seekers, which mostly appeared to have transpired in Christianity.

Encounter

This refers to the point of a crucial and dynamic interplay in religious conversion. It is often seen as ensuing between an advocate and a potential convert, strategically or not. The function of both the advocates and the potential converts play a pivotal role in the encounter stage.

In the case of Arunachal, Christianity and Charismatic movement, the advocates maintain a goal to expand the mission that they took up and decided to fulfil. Sometimes an advocate may be uncertain of who they should meet and how. Indeed, the inexperience of an advocate means that the nature of the task could also be misunderstood. To be an effective advocate at the encounter stage, one needs to be familiar with the local context and issues, and the place where they are about to meet potential converts. As Kahn and Greene assert, "the cultural, social, personal, and theological characteristics of advocate contribute importantly to the potential convert's experience."[34] Success or failure in the encounter stage solely depends upon an advocate and her/his potential convert's progression. Milton suggests that, "an advocate in conversion terms is an individual belonging to or representing the group to which a potential convert may turn, who engages in some form of interaction with the potential convert."[35] An advocate, in this context, can be defined as a person who acts as an agent of a religious movement in a particular community or society. However, in the context of the Pentecostal-Charismatic or Movements in Christianity, the work of the Holy Spirit is believed to be the primary power source of conversion, which works both with the advocate as well as the potential convert. Such an understanding can be concisely seen among the Charismatic Christians in Arunachal Pradesh precisely, who believe and publicly confess that every conversion, whether from another Christian group or from another religion, is the work of the Holy Spirit and for the improved transformation of that convert's life ahead.[36]

Interaction

This can be seen as the follow-up phase after an advocate encounters the potential convert, and while an expected convert is in the process of deciding. This also can be understood as a waiting period: whether a potential convert has fully decided to accept the change in their life as encouraged by the advocate. Here, there is a probability of some confronting-arguments. For example, while the potential convert is in the interaction phase, some religious orthodox may persuade the converts not to change and advise them to continue as they were. This would then nullify the process of the interaction stage. This could happen within the same religious group or by another religious group, or by some ethical ideals in the society which causes the potential convert to be in a position of belonging without believing.[37] There is also the possibility of a person becoming a convert without commitment.[38] However, in this case, an advocate can complete the stage by continuing in a relationship and play a role in the life of the convert and their family (continuing with the rituals and rhetoric already used),[39] which Rambo christened as the 'matrix of transformation.'[40]

Commitment

Advocates always expect those that they have helped to convert to follow their new life, post conversion. In many Christian traditions, it is vital for a new convert to demonstrate their commitment to their new faith. This commitment should be apparent to society through diverse activities and the involvement in different groups to which the convert has been recruited. Specifically, in the Charismatic Church movement, the convert's true decision can be identified from their active participation in one-time rituals, such as baptism, which can be seen as a symbol of surrendering oneself to live a life of faith in Christ Jesus, and then followed by daily ritual activities in the church community. As Kahn and Greene outline, "it is in the commitment phase that an experience of 'surrender' is found."[41] Some potential converts repudiate any sign of commitment as surrendering to a new way of life, which in reality have no connotations of conversion.

Consequences

Following a decision making, there will be a sense of the result, which could either be constructive or adverse. In the biblical meaning, the results of conversion will only be truly known after a new convert fully surrenders their life to God by dedicating their daily activities to be controlled by God's Spirit.[42] Travisano (1970) has suggested that a convert is recognisable by their piety.[43] The consequences of a conversion will depend upon the converts' commitment, whether weak or strong. These consequences may come sooner or later after the convert has made their commitment to keeping the ordinances of a particular religion through faith. Rambo identifies at least four major consequences based on historical, sociological, psychological and theological/religious impact.[44] In general, conversion scholars purport that the psychological causes are the most critical and are concerned with investigating on a personal bias what may have happened in the process of conversion. Religious consequences can be seen as the most crucial elements in the conversion process. There are times that consequences arise due to geographical reasons. For instance, if a Christian convert is from a Muslim-dominated place, then the cause of consequences may follow as per the majority religious group, for example, being forced from Islam or vice-versa. What the majority and minority religions are in any particular context can, at times, play a vital role in the event and process of conversion. As has been mentioned above, in such a context, a convert's commitment will potentially be tested. Some may give up on the idea of converting and return to their previous life, which in Christian terminology is called 'backsliding' or 'yielding again to the old nature of life.' The constant support to the convert by the advocate is imperative at such times, especially in attempts to convert those of other Christian movements or Islam, which are so-called true and life impacting religions that have a belief in both good and bad spirits in the world or universe.

Causes and Contributing Factors

In understanding Rambo's models of conversion, it becomes obvious that altering one's religion or faith has multiple reasons, which many single analyses may not correctly identify. As Milton suggests, "Beyond the question of definition, the literature preceding Rambo, particularly from the disciplines of sociology and psychology, reveals an almost ubiquitous preoccupation with the question of why people convert."[45]

The causes and contributing factors of conversion are varied, and indeed conversion is not only a multiple process but causes of conversion changes over time as the world (and particularly technology) changes. Furthermore, it can be seen that religious systems have also transformed their processes of organisation; some have been modified to fit in with the fast pace of change in the contemporary world, and these modifications have also included religious conversion.

This book attempts to use work from the sociology of religion to support empirical results, in this section, and will focus on some related social causes and contributing factors that are leading individuals, families, and indeed communities, to change and or re-direct their belief systems. David R. Hayward and Neal Krause identify that involvement in religious activities in society can help reduce anxieties associated with life uncertainties.[46] It is through religious and social involvement that there is inevitability of change and this brings a new development in their lives to a great extent.

In determining religious conversion as a social type, Snow and Machalek point out that there are at least six features of conversion that have commonly caused people to make a change to their religious beliefs in certain contexts. These are, being 'susceptible to cults,' 'religious seekers,' 'causal process models,' "physical aberrations, demonstration events…and group membership or participation," 'varying degrees of commitment' in the past belief or faith group, and 'radical change.'[47] These causes initially establish divisions over a period of time, adopting a master scheme on the new outlook. The iconic to new things, instead of analogy, embraces the master role with the new ideology, which Henri Gooren identifies as, time, space and mobility.[48]

Based on the sociological underpinning of conversion by Roger Straus, Gooren further argues, that whatever the situation, the first and foremost cause of conversion is evident by exclusively from person to person. However, Gooren disagrees with Straus on the 'brainwashing model,' arguing that Straus seems to have not precisely given a concrete reason how the 'brainwashing model' would have happened. Straus did identify that it is the individual who, owing to certain issues or crisis in their life, often makes the first move as a religious seeker, through "their social networks, and the mass media, gradually refining the nature of their quest, experimenting with a group..."[49] Through practical observation it is also evident that an individual can make a move to congenially influence both the family and the community. So, these six causes of conversion identified by Snow and Machalek, and then appraised by Gooren, are clearly causes that can develop from an individual and potentially contribute to further conversion of the family and society, often through social networks and social activities including media.

Furthermore, regarding Pentecostal-Charismatic conversion, one can identify that every individual is considered to be autonomous and independent of spiritual matters. In assessing Berger's conversion theory, Longo and Kim-Spoon have precisely argued that conversion in Pentecostal-Charismatic Christianity is often combined with enhanced or accelerated modernisation and secularisation, which, they suggest, "has given one man, one crucial ability beyond others: the ability to choose."[50] It can be observed that this reflected in the Charismatic Churches, whose spiritual and religious methods are entirely independent, and is also reflected in the practical forms of expression within the movements themselves, of which there are ample examples which has empirically seen in every ecclesial lives and services.

Active and Passive Conversion

The issue of conversion is not only discussed within the religious studies or theology, but also in sociology, psychology and anthropology. In all of these disciplines, it seems that the topic of conversion is a rousing one. Conversion has been discussed at length in both the psychology and the sociology of religion, which have conceptualised the idea of the active versus the passive in the politics of religious conversion, through investigating its cause and effects.[51]

According to Richardson, the notion of the active and the passive in the recruitment of new converts depends upon the power of an individual's discerning and determining the act that is sudden, dramatic and emotional; for instance, Paul's conversion experience. As Richardson while illustrating from a biblical perspective writes, "the Pauline experience is also often interpreted in cognitive terms. It was thought that what happened to Paul caused him to change his beliefs immediately and that behaviour's congruent with the new beliefs that had developed. Behaviours follow beliefs, then, in the traditional paradigm."[52] In the findings of both the social science and the psychology of religion, Richardson argues that although there are old (passive) and new (active) paradigm systems in the recruitment of new converts, both could be considered as traditional ways of looking at a model of conversion events. There are different arguments in these two traditions: the old tradition as passive and the new one as active. In the case of Paul, he was active in the persecution of the church when he had a sudden and dramatic experience of conversion that changed him once for all, which has been known as a passive conversion. Richardson explains that, "it was inexplicable in any terms except those that included an active agent, not under the convert's control. A powerful external agent over which Paul held no sway caused Paul to be converted."[53] This passivity of Paul at Damascus experienced in old paradigm seems to have influenced certain potential converts actively.

Gooren, in considering Richardson's terming of *conversion career* as multiple-event conversion and alongside Lofland and Stark, identifies three comprehensive dynamic models of conversion. With regards to the active, or new, conversion model, Gooren identifies a) prior socialisation, b) contemporary experiences and circumstances, and c) the opportunities available for problem and definitite solutions.[54] These three components of new conversion model are to be inevitably occurring through positive ties with members of the other religious or faith group.[55] This new, or active, model of conversion is sometimes reflected in human volition. Gooren outlines that "the 'new and active' conversion paradigm goes back to the definition of 'volitional conversion' by William James…as opposed to conversion by self-surrender."[56]

However, Lofland and Stark seemed to have had a mediating idea of conversion model that significantly linked the old and new contrasting models of conversion. This can be considered as a good alternative paradigm because it creates a bridge between the old and the new models, which Lofland and Stark referred to as the 'motivational' model and the 'push' model (pushing a person into conversion).[57] As far as Pentecostal-Charismatic conversion is concerned, one can observe a development of both the old or passive, and the new or active conversion models, which appear to have some countered with the secular humanism.

Looking at the diverse understandings, interpretations and analysis of contemporary religious conversion and the sociology of religion, it is clear that scholars have associated the majority of religious conversions with social crises and challenges. From this wide range meaning of conversion, conversion issues in Arunachal Pradesh also need to be understood within a wider spectrum, specifically conversion to Charismatic Church or Christianity.

Having done with the overall exploration of Christian religious conversion, I have considered the emergence of the Charismatic Christian movement's spirituality in Arunachal Pradesh in Chapter Four, where I have attempted to explore the context of that movement. The cause and effect of Charismatic or revival movement and or the spiritual syncretism by so-called Christian Spirituality through new conversion methods in the state is evident.

Endnotes

[1] Specifically, in the context of Arunachal Pradesh it is difficult to easily declare such converts have been taken place with the right work of the Holy Spirit as many Charismatics members appeared to have a very persuasive in the increment of their respective church members.

[2] It may be due to cultural and traditional factors, but I see quite a difference in the practice of worship in the Pentecostal-Charismatic Christian churches from place to place.

[3] ——————, 2012. *Oxford Dictionary of English*, Oxford: University Press.

[4] Starbuck, Diller E. 'A Study of Conversion' *The American Journal of Psychology*, Vol. 8, No. 2 (Jan., 1897), pp. 268-308 Published by: University of Illinois Press, http://www.jstor.org/stable/1410942 Accessed: 10-11-2015 23:48 UTC, 268.

[5] Lofland, John & Skonovd, Norman, 1981. 'Conversion Motifs', *Journal for the Scientific Study of Religion*, Wiley, 376.

[6] Halama, *Empirical Approach,* 187. Also, see Lofland & Skonovd 'Conversion Motifs', *Journal for the Scientific Study of Religion*, 377-379.

[7] O'Dea, Thomas F. 1966. *The Sociology of Religion*, New Jersey: PRENTICE Hall, INC, 55-56.

[8] Orsi, Robert, 1997. 'Everyday Miracles: The Study of Lived Religion,' in *Lived Religion America: Toward a History of Practice*, ed. Hall, David D., New Jersey: Princeton University Press, 8.

[9] O' Dea, *The Sociology of Religion*, 57.

[10] O' Dea, *The Sociology of Religion*, 60.

[11] In every individual's cause and effect of the convert or re-convert has some related social reasons in the context where conversion have been happened.

[12] Dawar, *Religious Conversion*, 60-1.

[13] Eriksen, Annelin, 2014. 'Sarah's Sinfulness Egalitarianism: Denied Difference, and Gender in Pentecostal Christianity', *The Anthropology of Christianity: Unity, Diversity, New Directions* (December 2014), pp. S262-S270 http://www.jstor.org, 261.

[14] Gender equal leadership in Christianity in Arunachal Pradesh is mostly practiced in the Charismatic movements.

[15] Bryant, Darrol, M. 1999. 'Conversion in Christianity: from without and within' in *Religious Conversion: Contemporary Practices and Controversy* (Ed. Lamb Christopher A. & M. Darrol Bryant), New York: CASSELL, 178.

[16] Marlett, Jeffrey D. 1997. *Conversion Methodology and the Case of Cardinal Newman,* http://www.domuni.eu/en/ accessed on 28.10.2015, 669.

[17] Halama, *Empirical Approach*, 186.

[18] Rambo, *Understanding Religious Conversion*, xi.

[19] Rambo, *Understanding Religious Conversion*, 2.

[20] In Arunachal Pradesh Converting from other faith has got no major issues but within the Christian faith group creates issues as observed and comments by the elite group.

[21] Conn, Walter, 1986, *Christian Conversion: A Developmental Interpretation of Autonomy and Surrender*, New Jersey: Paulist Press, 7.

[22] Gooren, *Religious Conversion*, 3.

[23] Gooren, *Religious Conversion*, 10.

[24] Gooren, Henri, 2010. 'Conversion Careers and Cultural Politics in Pentecostalism: Time, Space and Mobility in Four Continents' *PentecoStudies*, Equinox Publishing Ltd, 230.

[25] Peter, *Seeing Conversion Whole*, 234.

[26] Which means that no stage in the model should be understood to be the epicentre of conversion, but instead conversion can start from any of the seven stages due to the difference positions and lives of potential converts.

[27] Rambo, *Understanding Religious Conversion*, 17, 44. In Arunachal Pradesh, especially, when people convert to Charismatic Christianity, they explain that they had misunderstanding with the leaders and members of their

former church, and in some places family issues also affected their decision to change from one church or movement to another.

[28] Say for example, when a psychologist analyses the issues of conversion, one would say, he/she has a psychological problem which makes his/her mind inconsistent.

[29] Rambo, *Understanding Religious Conversion*, 44.

[30] Milton, *Understanding Pentecostal Conversion*, 94.

[31] Peter J. Kahn and A. L. Greene, 'Seeing Conversion,' 335.

[32] Rambo, *Understanding Religious Conversion*, 56-7.

[33] Milton, *Understanding Pentecostal Conversion*, 98.

[34] Peter and Greene, 'Seeing Conversion', 335.

[35] Milton, *Understanding Pentecostal Conversion*, 98.

[36] The work of the Holy Spirit in conversion in AP, however, is mainly believed to be the speaking in tongues and falling down of converts on the ground as an evident of true conversion taken place.

[37] Rambo, *Understanding Religious Conversion*, 68-9, 102.

[38] Milton, *Understanding Pentecostal Conversion*, 99.

[39] Peter and Greene, 'Seeing Conversion', 236.

[40] Rambo, *Understanding Religious Conversion*, 107.

[41] Peter and Greene, Seeing Conversion', 236.

[42] See Mathew chapter 16: 24 and John chapter 10:4.

[43] Snow, David A. and Machalek, Richard, 'The Convert as Social Type,' *Sociological Theory*, Vol. 1 (1983), 261-262.

[44] Rambo, *Understanding Religious Conversion*, 143-5.

[45] Milton, *Understanding Pentecostal Conversion*, 75.

[46] Hayward, David R. and Krause, Neal, 'Aging, Social Developmental, and Cultural Factors in Changing Patterns of Religious Involvement over a 32-Year Period: An Age–Period–Cohort Analysis of 80 Countries', *Journal of Cross-Cultural Psychology*, 2015, SAGE: Vol. 46(8) 979–995, 981.

[47] Snow and Machalek, 'The Convert as Social Type,' 262.

[48] Gooren, 'Conversion Careers', 243.

[49] Gooren, *Religious Conversion*, 25-6.

[50] Longo, Gregory S. and Kim-Spoon, Jungmeen, 2014. 'What Drives Apostates and Converters? The Social and Familial Antecedents of Religious Change Among Adolescents' *Psychology of Religion and Spirituality*, American Psychological Association, Vol. 6, No. 4, 285.

[51] Richardson, James T. 'The Active vs. Passive Convert: Paradigm Conflict in Conversion/Recruitment research', *Journal for the Scientific Study of Religion*, Vol. 24, No. 2 (Jun., 1985), pp. 163-179, Accessed: 02-11-2015 15:50 UTC.

[52] Richardson, *Psychology of Religion*, 165.

[53] Richardson, *Psychology of Religion*, 165.

[54] Richardson, *Psychology of Religion*, 166.

[55] Gooren, *Religious Conversion*, 34.

[56] Gooren, *Religious Conversion*, 34.

[57] Richardson, *Psychology of Religion*, 168.

Chapter 3
Emergence of Charismatic Christian Spirituality

Introduction

Arunachal Pradesh, although a remote, young and growing state in India is, nevertheless, certainly not detached from global events. Alongside developments in areas such as science and technology, economic and political growth, religious movements also are mushrooming all around the region. This chapter discusses primarily, the emergence of certain religious, spiritual groups or sects within Christianity, their origin and influence. Concomitantly, some evidence of inconsistencies in Christian doctrine amidst the fast-growing Christian churches in the region is investigated in this chapter.

Denominational Complexity

The findings of sociological and ethnographical studies on the nature of Christianity describe it as 'power hungry' with 'competitive contestants' cannot simply be ignored.[1] The multiplicity of denominations, even within some limited ecclesial congregations, is noticeable time and again in every Church movement. Even in a place such as Arunachal Pradesh, which has comparatively few Church denominations, there emerge to have arisen quite a number of Christian missions, church organisations, and spiritual groups, each claiming themselves to be the 'crusader,' 'reformer,' or force of 'spiritual awakening.'

Historically, the hunger for the spirit's power (within Christianity) seems to have started with the beginning of the Pentecostal and Charismatic movements in the early twentieth century as independent groups and individuals became hungry to depend upon the power of the Holy Spirit. As Cartledge notes, "at the beginning of the twentieth century there were some different evangelical revivals around the world, each with different characteristics, yet emphasising the work of the Holy Spirit and expressing aspects of the spirit's work through gifting's, signs and wonders and conversions."[2] Since then, Charismatic spirituality is growing significantly all over the world, influencing many established and mainstream Protestant Churches in less than a century. It has become, more or less, the tradition of almost every Charismatic church around the world. It could be argued that, whether a mainstream or Charismatic church mission, the mission strategy after the mid-twentieth century implicitly or explicitly are seen as the influences of the charismatic transcendental methodological mission. The Christian mission in Arunachal Pradesh became more effective only after the arrival of the more Charismatic type of mission between 1950 and 1970, especially around the state capital, Itanagar.[3] Cartledge is correct when he notes that, "new Churches have also emerged seeking to build different forms of church structures around a charismatically oriented spirituality."[4] In Arunachal Pradesh, it is specified that most of the churches' spiritual renewal movements are more Pentecostal-Charismatic oriented. For example, the Baptist churches, other Protestant Churches, and the Pentecostal Churches in the region, are related to one another. This Pentecostal-Charismatic oriented spiritual motivation is quite obviously noticeable through the oral and unwritten practices of daily worship and praise. Indeed, Smith asserts that, "there are thus now a highly significant proportion of Christians and churches termed as 'charismatic,' i.e. those that have a new emphasis on a dynamic experience of the Holy Spirit and the operation of the gifts of the Holy Spirit."[5] In most of the churches in Arunachal Pradesh, the minister or the preacher is expected to deliver the words of God on Sunday without a manuscript. Indeed, total dependence on a written manuscript by preacher would create dissatisfaction to the congregation.[6] Therefore, this relates to how historians of Pentecostal-Charismatic Christianity have termed the beginning of Pentecostalism as the pristine era of the early church as recorded in the book of Acts. The significance of communicating the theological understandings of early Christian spirituality, the continuity with the original New Testament Christianity and the early Church's method of worship is obvious.[7]

Yet, on the other hand, there have been some misconceptions among churches in the area in which this study is based, due to confusing spiritual recruitments. The first misconception caused due to confusion in spiritual conscriptions seen, as every denomination having their Church mission strategy with the attitude of membership increment. The membership drive within each mission organisation appeared to have a sense of competitive in its work both substantially and spiritually.[8]

The second distinctive misconception, which can sometimes cause stern disagreements between the Pentecostal-Charismatic church and the mainstream Protestant church are the issues of speaking in tongues, seeing visions, and uttering prophecies. The system of worship in the Pentecostal-Charismatic churches is oral or mostly non-manuscript preaching of the words of God has helped every bit. However, the excessive seeing of visions, prophecies, and speaking in tongues during intensive hours of prayer is quite contradictory to the two-fold Spiritual movement.[9] These types of spiritual movements in the state's Charismatic churches have been criticised by some of other faiths who regard the Charismatic Christian church as an 'immature religious movement in the state.'[10] This often appears to be a hurdle for some Christian missions and links to what Bearak Max expresses:

> Tribal religion has adapted some of the modern forms of worship in response to its dwindling followers. Within the past five years, locals say, the Donyi-Polo faith has become more institutionalized in its practices, as its leaders have realized that it suffers from being seen as a disorganized and a timeworn default religion.[11]

The third distinctive confusion that arises because of the complex Charismatic church movements is that by its nature it has a sort of individual uniqueness with regards to its spiritual characteristics, while at the same time, their use of the mainstream church's method of administration, and other features of its mission, makes them indistinguishable. Alongside other fragmentation features, such as the so-called 'experience of the power of the Holy Spirit,' through speaking in tongues, it is noticeable that the ecclesial organisation system is somewhat a random effort. Bernice Martin identifies that, "comparative research on worldwide Pentecostalism may well achieve more by clarifying what is distinctive in the Pentecostals' experience and pattern of conversion rather than by refining a model of 'conversion careers' that can have universal relevance."[12] One can see how the disorganised nature of Charismatic Christianity challenges the movement to turn back somewhat to the mainstream church in the society, to help establish themselves as an organised movement. Accurately commenting on the issue, Simon Chan notes that, "on the one hand, they [the Pentecostal movement] want to maintain their distinctive experience and this often means having to define it against the mainstream interpretation. On the other hand, they feel the need of establishment to their orthodox credentials by identifying themselves with some larger body."[13] Chan's identification suitably reflects the context in Arunachal Pradesh, although the Charismatic church often disapproves of the spiritual nature of the mainstream churches (for example, the Baptists and the Catholic Church). However, they still look to replicate the established churches' methods of officiating and administrative system. They frequently want to associate with the mainstream church to make their services better known, although they still consider their movement to be the most spiritually distinctive. Despite this, however, it can be seen that if churches in Arunachal Pradesh can all work together, both in the form of more unified theological understanding of Christian ministry and progress of contextualising Christian mission would be beneficial in evangelising and furthering the mission in the state as a whole.[14]

Finally, an exceptional phenomenon, commonly practiced by both the mainstream church and the Pentecostal-Charismatic church in Arunachal Pradesh, is the divine healing method of ministry, such as revivals and healing crusades. These types of spiritual awakening programmes are regularly organised by all churches in the state, such as the Christian Revival Church, Pentecostals, Baptists and Catholics alike. It is remarkable to see the Catholic Church, which traditionally considered being spiritually moribund, have initiated the same in the recent years.[15] One can assert that, if there is something that might bring the spirit of unity to Christianity - not only in Arunachal Pradesh but all over the world - it might well be the divine healing ministry. Through healing ministries, true love and care for fellow human beings is manifested within Christianity. As Candy Gunther Brown succinctly affirms:

> Most practitioners prefer the term "divine healing" because it emphasizes that God's love, rather than merely human faith or an impersonal spiritual force, is the source of healing; it underscores the perceived need for supernatural intervention instead of implying that faith is a natural force that can be manufactured by human will; and it emphasizes that the object of faith, not simply the degree of faith or spirituality, matters in healing.[16]

In accordance with Gunther Brown's observation above, we see in Arunachal Pradesh that the singular most common characteristic of all churches is their use of healing ministry. When people in this region see any form of healing crusade or prayer, they don't usually question which denomination is hosting the event (except some conservative mainline church adherents who neither believe in healing nor encourage such ministry). Details of a Christian Revival Church healing crusade in Itanagar, Arunachal Pradesh, on November 16th 2014 is an example of this type of event:

> Thousands of believers from the state and other parts of the country participated in a three-day 'festival of healing' organized by the Arunachal Pradesh Christian Revival Church, Papum Pare District, at IG Park, Itanagar. The festival, which began on 14th November, was aimed at spreading the healing power of God, and to encourage people to follow the path of peace and brotherhood.[17]

One can comprehend such practices of healing ministries in the region as congruent to those exhibited in African Pentecostal churches. Cephas N. Omengyo argues that healing is commonly emphasised in the African Charismatic Christian movement, who consider it to be the primary source of success in the Pentecostal and Charismatic context.[18] Along with Bauman, the healing ministry in Arunachal Pradesh can be considered as a denominational 'interbreeding.' Bauman aptly identifies the complexity of evangelicalism and Pentecostalism in India, yet in many places similarities exist as "a hybrid swarm of interbreeding, backcrossing, and intraspecific hybrids" species, which is undeniably evident in the Arunachal Pradesh unquestionably.[19] However, according to Shaibu's argumentative observation concerning the whole of the Indian Charismatic-Pentecostal movement, healing ministries were originally practiced earlier within the mainline church's spiritual renewal movements before erupting in popularity in the Pentecostal movement of the early 20th century.[20]

Another common practice seen in the twofold Charismatic movement is gender-segregation of seating system in the church where men and women sit on opposite sides of the church, along with most of the women wearing white veils. Unlike in the Western churches, in Arunachal Pradesh one would hardly see a wife and husband sitting together in the church for the Sunday worship service. This could also be identified as a global Pentecostal-Charismatic church practice. As George R. Saunders, while studying Pentecostal churches in Italy, informs us, "men and women sit on opposite sides of the church, and women wear white veils during the service. The service is dominated by men, although women do participate actively with prayers and testimonies."[21]

Market Metaphors

The next section, looks at the market metaphors used to describe the global Pentecostal-Charismatic movement the market model of Pentecostal and Charismatic churches, but relatively to look into it briefly as it relates to the context of Arunachal Pradesh. Bernice Martin, in discussing Pentecostal conversion and the limits of the market metaphor, argues that although this fast-growing movement appears to have attracted considerable numbers of people almost all over the whole world, simultaneously it also has "obscured the importance of the transformative process in conversion."[22] As Martin rightly asserts, it is often ostensibly evident, even among the least Charismatic of the churches, when there is too much of an ecstatic emphasis in a religious organisation. This is undeniably identifiable, even in Arunachal Pradesh, where Christianity as a whole is still at a very young and growing stage. However, owing to the Charismatic movements in the state, the true nature of religious transformation is rather difficult to ascertain, and is more controversial conversion events which relates to Henri Gooren accurately observes and have classified as "micro, meso, and macro levels," conversion.[23] Past analyses from the sociology of religion, such as the old and monopolies model, in which religion will gradually disappear from human societies, can be seen as recurring with the emergence of the Pentecostal-Charismatic movement across the world. As Gooren further classifies, "the micro-level involves the supposed rational actor, the meso-level has a concern with the competitive religious organisation, while the macro-level deals with the religious market as part of a greater religious economy."[24] As far as Arunachal Pradesh is concerned, the first and the third levels of Gooren's classification have not been very evident. However, the second level, which is concerned with the competition between churches, is quite obvious as membership within a denominational group is often fluid. For example, in one village of Arunachal Pradesh, where a Baptist church was established fifty years ago, and the village is now 95% Christian.[25] In that same village, the Christian Revival Church attempted to establish another church, claiming that the village needed a great revival. One can also see the meso level model of conversion as active in the same way in the state, which sometimes creates confusion and controversial contexts in which the Gospel was supposed to be proclaimed peacefully aiming to the unreached places. Instead, as Gooren further argues, "it seems to me that churches also compete with attractions of their doctrine, their rules of conduct, their particular use of missionaries, their general evangelizing efforts, and the strength of their organization."[26]

Regarding religious economy, which both Gooren and Martin have discussed at length, this is not very evident in Arunachal Pradesh, except some within their own churches who try to persuade others to give money for infrastructures and mission funds. However, the relationship between the political and social approach, for the greater recognition of church and its movement, has been often been initiated by the Charismatic-oriented churches of the region.[27]

Spiritual Syncretism

History and sociology prove that religious syncretism has been a phenomenon throughout the history of humanity. All religions of the globe, both major and minor, have undeniably been noted by historians as, in some way or another, syncretic. Syncretism occurs because throughout human history generations have continued to relocate, and therefore cultural context and customs also change. Christianity and Islam, the world's most popular religions, are not quite 'pure' doctrinally and theologically. Alongside religious 'push and pull within' human societies, simultaneously, they attempt to harmonise different religious beliefs seems to have taken place, often spontaneously. On the one hand, such syncretism can be seen as bringing unification to particular societies through a blending of religious attitudes. On the other hand, it could also be seen as having produced confusion and struggles between religions around the world. An example of this confusion could be the Jewish diaspora and the Hellenistic world. As Frank Bryon argues, "the Jews of the diaspora were widely scattered over the Hellenistic world; wherever they settled their monotheism attracted proselytes from amongst the best type of men; why should they have had not converted the world to Judaism?"[28] One can comprehend, as long as some religious actions are practiced in a manner of beatitude, there is the potential to attract other people who are non-religious or people of other faiths.

It is clear then, from the above, that religious or spiritual syncretism has occurred and re-occurred throughout human history. The focus here will be on some aspects of spiritual syncretism within Christian spirituality, with special reference to the context in Arunachal Pradesh, where in some places this syncretism has been defined as a battle between 'spirituality versus Spiritism' among the Charismatic movements.[29] Winnifred Kirkland, while discussing the concept of 'spirituality versus Spiritism' argues that this dualism is in many places, confused and not only creates conflict within Christian spirituality, but also brings psychological issues into one's spiritual journey.[30] In Kirkland's understanding, issues caused between spirituality and Spiritism is due to the misleading messages of some spiritual leaders, which place too much focus on dreams and visions. When some Charismatic leaders tend to contact the correct Spirit of God through spiritual discourses, misguidance can occur at points where the intersection of the dead spirit depicts the situation as right. This type of incidence can occur frequently when a spiritual person is wanting to relate spiritual blessings into materialism very often.[31] This interconnection of good and bad spirits often occurs among the Charismatic spiritual movements in the tribal states/regions, and there have been some reports of incidences, often leading to division within a family or between spouses. As Kirkland further outlines, "there remains to divide the people who do believe it into those who think and those who don't."[32]

Another conspicuous spiritual syncretism among Charismatic Christianity in Arunachal Pradesh, as mentioned above, is traditional spirituality with Charismatic Christian spirituality. Traditionally, since time immemorial, there has been a practice of ensuring an extraordinary vision by the priest through ritual chanting and utterances. At such times the priest can picture the unseen and the unknown spiritual world when he chants with a deep utterance, which other people cannot easily comprehend.[33] People believe that through these utterances and ritual chanting, the priest is connecting to supernatural contacts, and moreover, that the priest subsequently gets power from certain "forces, gods, spirits, ghosts or demons."[34] Apparently, a similar type of practice has repeatedly been found among Charismatic church leaders, not only among the Pentecostal or Revival christians, but also among the Charismatic spiritual movements in the mainstream churches as well. Such evidence is phenomenon from some of the Charismatic church's spiritual practices, where one can recognise that, after many hours of excessive prayer and the uttering of prophecy and foretelling of an event yet to happen, the leader sometimes, unhesitant to reveal the hidden issues within the family of church members, thereby creating misunderstandings within the family.[35] Because of such incidences, some observant criticise Christian spirituality as being a dual spirituality or a mix-up of Christianity with the cultic spirituality of the ancient near east.[36] As Schwab, in his study entitled, *Is Christianity a Moral Code of Religion?* argues,[37] although the disciples and the first followers of Jesus were taught by their master to keep the morals of true Christian spirituality, as they came across to other spirituality linked to some ancient belief and cults, they seemed to have misled by them, "You may conceive the followers have come under their influence. They may have been carried away by this spiritual wave, and so Christianity may have become tinged with a foreign colouring. They, therefore, let go what was essential in Christ's teaching and seized what was merely accidental and traditional."[38]

A similar type of practice is palpable in many of Arunachal Pradesh Charismatic church movements. Indeed, there have been some incidents of people having been burnt to death by such excessive Charismatic spiritual groups, because the victim was thought to resist the work of the Holy Spirit.[39]

It is obvious that the emergence of Charismatic movements in this region has had both advantages and disadvantages for the religious state of affairs of the region as a whole. It should be noted that one of the advantages is an awakening of spirituality, or religiosity, both in Christianity and also in other faiths, which has initiated a progression and reformulation of religious systems in various forms in each religious group of the state including indigenous faith.[40] It may perhaps be concomitantly arguable that one of the disadvantages is an increasing doctrinal and pneumatological confusion within ecclesial level whereby resulting of spiritual or religious syncretism which will need to be rectified in due course has been realised. Preceding the emergence of Charismatic spirituality, it is also essential to consider the areas of origin and the foundation of the Charismatic movements in the region that has evidently classified as a Charismatic motivational factor in the context of Christian spirituality, which follows in the next section.

The Roots of Charismatic Movements in Arunachal Pradesh

The Pentecostal-Charismatic movement is a well-known global phenomenon in the modern history of Christianity. Before focusing on the origin of the Charismatic movements in the region, it is important to look into the early development of the movement globally, a movement that has reached far-flung corners of the world in less than a century. Although the origin of the Pentecostal-Charismatic movement has its roots in the early twentieth century, evidence substantiates that there were multiple precursors of evangelical Christian movements around the world which had a great impact in the eruption of Pentecostal-Charismatic in the early twentieth century. As Joel Robbins notes:

> Pentecostalism's roots lie in the Protestant evangelical tradition that grew out of the eighteenth-century, Anglo-American revival movement known as the Great Awakening. Evangelical Christianity, which includes such denominations as Methodists and Baptists, is marked by its emphasis on conversion. People are not born into the evangelical faith but must "voluntarily" choose it on the basis of powerful conversion experiences (often glossed as being "born again"). Because evangelicals believe this experience is available to everyone, they strongly emphasise the importance of evangelistic efforts to convert others.[41]

As rightly identified and delineated by Robbins above phrase, in this, manner from the origin of Global evangelical Charismatic

Christianity and throughout its history, it has been the fastest growing spiritual movement and has reached almost all corners of the globe. Similarly, one can see that Charismatic Christianity in every nation or region has implicitly or explicitly developed from the foundations of the mainline church. Indeed, in Arunachal Pradesh, it can be seen that the Charismatic movement, in its inception, was based on the mainstream church of Baptist and other Protestant denominations' spiritual renewal impact.[42]

Naga Origins

As far as the Charismatic church around the globe is concerned, the movement is very much focused on the spiritual aspects of an individual, rather than placing importance on the educational qualifications of church leaders. In Charismatic Christianity, therefore, it can be observed that lay leaders dominate, and theological training is considered to be a stumbling block for church growth and mission strategies alike. In this regard, the arguments of John Corrie are correct, when he writes that, "ironically, some of the most successful Pentecostal pastors and leaders are people with very little formal theological education. Their priority is more on their ability to cast out demons and the spiritual gifts of the leaders than on their intellectual skills."[43]

The Charismatic Christian movement in the northeast part of India in general, and Arunachal Pradesh in particular, is often understood as a movement that has links to Naga people, the movement which started sometime in the 1970s and 1980s.[44] According to the observation of various elderly people in Nagaland, Christian Revival Church was founded by a group of Christians who left the Baptist Church, owing to what was considered to be a moribund spirituality within the mainline church during the 70s and 80s.[45] Nevertheless, recent historical research of Christianity in Nagaland shows that, in 1972, revival movements were experienced by all churches in that region. These revivals started at a time when Billy Graham came to Nagaland and preached about the necessity of revival in the Church and the need to continue proclaiming the gospel of Jesus Christ around the world.[46] As far as the history of Nagaland is concerned, the 1970s and 1980s were period when horrendous political, social and religious situations occurred, owing to unsettled issues between the Indian National government and the Naga nationalistic movements, who were pursuing independence.[47] Relatively, Chad M. Baumann, compares even the southern Indian Pentecostal-Charismatic movement significantly started their mixed Charismatic Evangelical movement in the period of the 1960s and 70s, which had spread all over India.[48]

Using recent ministry data from the Ministry of Nagaland, Fernando Faustin, writing in *Revival Magazine reports* states:

> Today they have 98% Christians, mainly from Baptist denominations. A young Youth invited me with a Mission (YWAM) leader based in Nagaland to bring the message of the Father's Heart and give people the opportunity to know more about the move of the Holy Spirit that we experienced in Toronto.[49]

According to Faustin's understanding and experience concerning the work of the Holy Spirit, there is a genus of automated networking of the spirit which links all around the world. Spirituality through the proper Holy Spirit works of God is indeed indisputably believable and it authenticates the doctrine of pneumatological understanding even in the ecclesial levels.

Christian Revival Church

The above brief outlook and the overall practical observations on the origin of Charismatic church in Arunachal Pradesh have relatively identified that the origin and foundation of Charismatic movements in the region are implicitly or explicitly linked to Naga Charismatic Christianity initiated by the mainline church's evangelical revival movement prior to the Christian Revival Church, which is in itself a specific offshoot of the Baptist renewal movements of the 1970s and 1980s. As far as Arunachal Charismatic church is concerned, it is not feasible in finding any original documents or literature concerning the accurate originality, as nothing has yet been written about it. However, the souvenirs of silver jubilee celebrations of both the Arunachal Pradesh Christian Revival Church Council (APCRCC) and the Christian Revival Church in Itanagar in recent years have publicized, to a certain extent, how and when it ignited. Therefore, the discussion are based on the origins of the APCRCC in this section on reports from their souvenir booklets. These silver jubilee celebrations were conducted in 2012 (APCRCC) and 2014 (CRC) respectively, which states:

> It is to be put on record that the revival movement first started with the Holy Spirit stirring the people at Silli Baptist Church during the first Revival Crusade from 9th to 13th January 1981, where Rev. Bielieu Shuya was one of the speakers. It was followed by Christian Revival Church establishment at Tengabari, Naharlagun, Leku and so on.[50]

Some elderly Baptist Church members commented that many of the early Church Revival Church members drifted to the new movement from Baptist and Catholic churches. The above quotation from the souvenir booklet also affirms that the revival movement was an offshoot of a Baptist Church revival crusade in Nagaland. The authentic origin of the Charismatic Church in the state can also be traced back to the Baptist Church's movements of spiritual renewal as have partly been explained above.[51]

The two silver jubilee celebrations committee members undoubtedly stated the emergence and existence of APCRCC as a whole were a genuine source of approval in regard to the movement. According to APCRCC and CRC, a wider understanding of Christian spirituality and its influence of spiritual awakening to the whole state in multiple areas arrived by means of the movements through Christian Revival Church.[52] The political leaders and business bureaucrats of the region have been significantly encouraged to join in the mission of God, not necessarily as full-time workers but in various capacities, in spreading the word of God and establishing churches all around the area in possible conducts.

Although there are complexities in tracing out the origins of the Charismatic movement in Arunachal Pradesh authentically, but an attempt has been made in the preceding chapter to make it compatible.

Endnotes

[1] Haynes, Naomi. 'Affordances and Audiences Finding the Difference Christianity Makes.' *Current Anthropology*, Vol. 55, No. S10, The Anthropology of Christianity: Unity, Diversity, New Directions (December 2014), The University of Chicago Press http://www.jstor.org/stable/10.1086/678285. Accessed: 11/11/2015, 358.

[2] Cartledge, *Testimony in the Spirit*, 2.

[3] Neelam, Taram, 2008. *A Glimpses into Arunachal Christianity*, Guwahati: Nillgrim Press, 37.

[4] Cartledge, Mark J. 2006. *Encountering the Spirit: Charismatic Tradition*, London: Longman and Todd Ltd., 19.

[5] Smith, Graham R. 2011. *The Church Militant: A Study of "Spiritual Warfare" in the Anglican Charismatic Renewal*, (PhD Thesis) Birmingham: University of Birmingham, 1.

[6] Whoever is preaching at a Sunday worship service is expected to speak freely without depending on the written word. The followers of this Christian movement firmly believe that the words of God should be spoken by being inspired by God's spirit at the moment of speaking.

[7] Burgess, Stanley M. 'Cutting the Taproot: The Modern Pentecostal Movement and its Traditions', *Spirit and Renewal: Essays in Honour of J. Rodman Williams*, (Ed. John Christopher Thomas, Rick D. Moore & Steven J. Land, 1994), Sheffield: Sheffield Academic Press, 60.

[8] Nyishi Baptist Church Council, one of the largest Baptist mission oorganisations (and one in which I am a staff member), has just recently finished a mission project named 'Mission 2015'. This 10-year project was initiated in 2005 and formed a strategic plan to establish one church in each village without having any consultation with other church denominations in the state or even with the local ethnic groups.

In addition, the Christian Revival Church of Arunachal Pradesh also has a mission project to establish one rrevival church in each village.

[9] At times, in some Charismatic-Pentecostal Churches, revival conferences or crusades, they openly prophesy against the mainstream church and mission activities.

[10] It reportedly said, in some of the Charismatic-Pentecostal church crusade or conference they openly prophesy against the mainline churches and their mission activities as humanly effort. This is why the mainline church elders consider Charismatic movement as immature type of Christianity in AP.

[11] Max, Barak, 2014. 'A Competition for Converts in Arunachal Pradesh', *India ink, Notes on the World Largest Democracy*, http://india.blogs.nytimes.com/2014/02/04/a-competition-for-converts-in-arunachal-pradesh/ Accessed on 09.11.2015.

[12] Martin, Bernice, 2006. 'Pentecostal Conversion and the Limits of the Market Metaphor', *Exchange*, Vol.35(1), pp.61-91 [Peer Reviewed Journal], 82.

[13] Chan, Simon, 2000. *Pentecostal Theology and the Christian Spiritual Tradition*, Sheffield: Sheffield Academic Press, 11.

[14] The largest Christian Revival Church (CRC) of Arunachal Pradesh is slowly integrating the organisational system of the mainline Church in the state and they have started following the presidential and secretariat systems, which until recently they rejected.

[15] On one Sunday in January 2015, I saw crowds of people all around the Catholic Church campus. When I went nearby and asked people what was going on, someone told me that a healing prayer service was underway, and that it had started after the Sunday devotional service. I was very surprised to hear this.

[16] Brown, Candy Gunther. 2011., *Global Pentecostal and Charismatic Healing*, [online] Oxford Scholarship Online, http://www.myilibrary.com/ Accessed on 8.11.2015, 4-5.

[17] Eastern Sky Media, http://easternskymedia.co.in/tag/town-baptist-church/ Accessed on 16-11-2015.

[18] Omengyo, Cephas N. 'New Wine in an Old Wine Bottle? Charismatic Healing in the Mainline Churches in Ghana' in *Global Pentecostal and Charismatic Healing*, (Ed. Brown, Candy Gunther, 2011), New York: Oxford University Press, 236.

[19] Bauman, 'Who Are India's Pentecostals?', 3.

[20] Shaibu, Abraham. *Ordinary Indian Pentecostal Christology*, (PhD Thesis, 2011) University of Birmingham, 110-111.

[21] Saunders, George R. 1995. *The crisis of presence in Italian Pentecostal conversion*, (American Ethnologist, Vol. 22, No. 2 May 1995), pp. 324-340, http://www.jstor.org/stable/646705. Accessed: 21-09-2015 18:24 UTC, 325.

[22] Martin, Bernice, 2006. 'Pentecostal Conversion and the Limits of the Market Metaphor', *Exchange* Vol.35 (1), pp.61-91, 61.

[23] Gooren, Henri, 'The Religious Market Model and Conversion: Towards a New Approach', *Exchange*, Volume 35, Issue 1, pages 39 – 60 Publication Year: 2006, 40.

[24] Gooren, 'The Religious Market', 40.

[25] The name of this village is Talo where the first Baptist Church of Nyishi, my own ethnic group, was established in 1962. Now very few families are non-Christian.

[26] Gooren, 'The Religious Market', 47.

[27] Engaging with the related social and political matters in the society is often initiated by the Pentecostal-Charismatic type of churches. It may be because they want to convey the whole of the Gospel of Jesus Christ to the community as a whole.

[28] Jevons, Bryon F. 'Hellenism and Christianity', *the Harvard Theological Review*, Vol. 1, and No. 2 (April 1908), 172, Accessed: 13-11-2015.

[29] There are some individuals who practice some sort of special prayer which is offered to people, and in which they predict things what are going to happen. These are not exactly the prophecies or visions that we find in the Bible, and yet these tellers seem to receive their predictions from the spirit of God or Jesus.

[30] Kirkland, Winnifred, 'Spirituality versus Spiritism: A Confession of Faith', in *The North American Review*, Vol. 213, No. 782 (Jan., 1921), http://www.jstor.org/stable/25120660. Accessed: 13-11-2015 14:46 UTC, 83-5.

[31] Kirkland, 'Spirituality versus Spiritism', 84.

[32] Kirkland, 'Spirituality versus Spiritism', 85.

[33] My father, who passed away in 1986, was a village priest and had this type of gift which I observed in my teenage years.

[34] Bhagabati, C. A., 'Indigenous Faiths and Customs: some Observations' in *Indigenous Faith and Practices of the Tribes of Arunachal Pradesh*, (Ed. M. C. Behera and S. K. Chaudhuri, 1998, 2004), Itanagar: Himalayan Publishers, 1.

[35] For example, in 2007, at one of the 'prayer towers', which are run by a Charismatic Baptist church group, a prayer leader (who is known in that group as a 'counsellor') was praying for a female client. After a long time of prayer, he mistakenly uttered a secret of the client's family, which caused a rift between the woman and her husband. Up to now, this family's problems, which were caused by this revelation, is yet to be restored.

[36] There are multiple issues that occurred in different places even around the capital city of Itanagar. Recently it was reported that there is another prayer tower, called 'The Second Coming Prayer Centre', where after healing prayers for sick people, the prayer leader stamps on the sick people's bodies, with the intention of forcing Satanic spirits to leave the body of the patient.

[37] Schwab, Henry L. 'Is Christianity a Moral Code a Religion?' in *The Harvard Theological Review*, Vol. 3, No. 3 (Jul., 1910), Cambridge University Presshttp://www.jstor.org/stable/1507010. Accessed: 15-11-2015 01:31 UTC, 271-2.

[38] Schwab, Henry L. 'Is Christianity a Moral Code a Religion?' in *The Harvard Theological Review*, Vol. 3, No. 3 (Jul., 1910), Cambridge University Presshttp://www.jstor.org/stable/1507010. Accessed: 15-11-2015 01:31 UTC, 271-2.

[39] It is reported that in 2007, in one of the most remote areas of AP, a woman was burnt alive by a Christian spiritual group just because she refused to confess her sins in front of that group. This information had been kept secret by the villagers, as they felt that this could cause problems for all other Christians in the state.

[40] One can see that, due to Charismatic movements, the traditional religion of the region has been reformulated as Donyi-Poloism. Within Christianity, almost every denomination has awakened their spiritual activities.

[41] Robbins, Joel, 'The Globalization of Pentecostal and Charismatic Christianity', in *Annual Review of Anthropology*, Vol. 33 (2004), http://www.jstor.org/stable/25064848. Accessed: 16-11-2015 16:24 UTC, 119-20.

[42] Some of the pastors that I have met in the Christian Revival Churches were Baptist Church members some 5-10 years ago.

[43] Corrie, John, 'Theological Education in Latin America: Bolivia as a Case Study' in *Transformation* 2015, Vol. 32(4) 281–293, trn.sagepub.com. Accessed on 17/11/2015, 282.

[44] http://churchgrowthmodelling.blogspot.co.uk/2015/04/nagaland-revival-1976-1982.html. Accessed on 17-11-2015.

[45] Between 1995 and 1999 I was studying my Bachelor of Theology at Trinity Theological College, Nagaland. Some elderly mainstream Church leaders used to explain to the college students about the Charismatic Christians in Nagaland who were formerly members of the established church in the state.

[46] http://churchgrowthmodelling.blogspot.co.uk/2015/04/nagaland-revival-1976-1982.html. Accessed on 17/11/2015, 282.

[47] Thomas, John. Church and the Formation of Naga Political Identity, 1918-1997, (PhD Thesis, 2010, reviewed by Papori Bora), Guwahati: Jawaharlal Nehru University, Centre for Historical Studies. http://dissertationreviews.org/archives/6663. Accessed on 21/11/2015.

[48] Baumann, Chad M. 2015, 'Who are India's Pentecostals?' *Oxford Scholarship Online*, Oxford: University Press. 5.

[49] Fernando, Faustin, 'Ministry in Nagaland' in *Revival Magazine: A Spiritual Alive Perspective on Christian Living*, http://revivalmag.com/article/ministry-nagaland. Accessed on 17-11-2015.

[50] Dodum, Sama, 2012. *Souvenir: APCRCC Silver Jubilee (1987 – 2012)*, Naharlagun, Eureka Offset & Imaging Systems, 12.

[51] My informal interviews and conversations with two mainline church leaders and members helped me to understand the origins of Charismatic Church movement in Arunachal Pradesh.

[52] Bomjen, Jiken, 2014. *Souvenir*, CRC-ESS Sector Itanagar, Itanagar: Amar Bajwa, 22.

Chapter 4

The Present Scenario in the Churches in Arunachal Pradesh

Having explored the emergence and origins of the Charismatic movement in Arunachal Pradesh briefly, this chapter will deal with the empirical research fieldwork carried out, particularly at the Christian Revival Church, Itanagar in December 2015 and January 2016 respectively. Interlocutors included two other Baptist organisation church leaders and believers from Apatani Baptist Association (ABA), and the Nyishi Baptist Church Council (NBCC)). Some significant church leaders and members from both the aforementioned church organisations have considerably supported, specifically, in regard to the assessment on progressive unity as church movement in the state.

In this book, the focus has largely been made on the impact of practical theological experiences through daily participation in the church which significantly resulted on development of social transformation. On the one hand, it is evident that after conversion to Charismatic church/Christianity as in church claimants, such as the Christian Revival Church, and with Charismatic effort, certain social transformations have evidentially been experienced by those converts. The converts' claimed that there are two evidential experience brought by conversion to the Charismatic church, particularly, and Christianity in general on the social transformation, such as, healing and speaking in tongues. On the other hand, there is a certain doctrinal contradiction, predominantly, with regard to the water and spirit baptism apprehended agreement between the mainline church and the Charismatic movement, the one that will be discussed below. Incorporating scholars' understanding of speaking in tongues, the healing aspect, and its significant impact on social transformation has been reflected in the findings and analysis of this research. This chapter intends to focus on speaking in tongues and healing of physical ailments through Charismatic church movements, which certainly are the most dominant factors of shifting from one church group to another of conversion career effects with other faiths. The two major impacts of the Charismatic church movements in Arunachal Pradesh have been epitomized in the picture of Christian Revival Church and certain Charismatic evangelical oriented Baptist church in the region.

Some of the findings behind the conversion

The findings and analysis on the role of speaking in tongues in the case study congregation are primarily based on their answers. These members are considered to be the key figures of the church, and their conversions seemed to mean a lot to their church as well. As Pastor Tap Taluk stated, "these leaders and members to whom we have distributed the questions are the active leaders and members of this church in multiple ways, not only for spiritual growth but all-round developments as well."[1] Most of the answers to the question, 'why did you affiliate to Christian Revival Church?', expressed something along the lines of not finding any spiritual satisfaction in their former church. For example, one respondent wrote that, "The Church I attended for more than 20 years was a monotonous religious one, on Sunday worships only. There were no any spiritual renewal activities for the members/believers."[2] Similar sentiments were reflected in answers from other believers who had changed their denomination, especially those who had moved from the Baptist Church to Christian Revival Church. With regards to the issue of shifting affiliations, my critical analysis, therefore, concluded that changing from one denomination to another, mainly happened because, as a believer of God, the person that made that change longed for spiritual satisfaction.[3] These affiliated members from another Church to Christian Revival Church were felt satisfied with their spiritual hungriness being in the newly affiliated group.

According to their answers, only 10% of respondents were formerly members of the Catholic Church. The reason behind this lesser number of people who have shifted from the Catholic Church is because there are less Catholic churches in the region, particularly, Itanagar, the capital area. As one elderly member of Christian Revival Church stated, "There are few Catholic Church in Itanagar, where attendants on Sunday are less, however, more in the rural areas."[4] Some converts from the Catholic Church openly stated that they know that Catholicism is not Christian; instead they considered it as commercial or Semi-government Company and organisation of Arunachal Pradesh. "We do not fully consider Catholic as Christian; because they join all sorts of local and national festivals, which a Christian should not participate for example, Nyokum Festival of Nyishi tribe. Of course, they are experts in communal and educational works."[5] 60% of converts had previously followed indigenous religions and the DP, as mentioned in the introduction.

Social Transformation through the Conversion Movement

C. Nunthara says "change normally takes the form of transformation, its movement is from a simple to relatively complex form of organisations."[6] I am aware of delving into the complete transformation of society, however, few impacts of Christianity through conversion/change in a practical manner of life, in the levels of individual, family and communal life.

Role of Speaking in Tongues in the Church

Since its emergence in the early 20th century, speaking in tongues has remained a key practice in the Pentecostal-Charismatic movement. Indeed, glossolalia appeared to be at the foundation of the movement, ignited as it was in different places around the globe (albeit Azusa Street was declared as the locus of the movement's ability to overcome racial segregation).[7] Looking into the context of India, Gary B. McGee notes that similar incidences occurred in several places in India, such as Pandita Ramabai's Mukti Mission in Kedgoan, southern India, and at Khassia Hills in northeast India, both of which preceded Azusa Street.[8] From the beginning of the Pentecostal-Charismatic movement, one can see that speaking in tongues has been given a lot of attention, and understood to be the primary factor in conversion to Pentecostalism. Furthermore, this is reflected in the context of conversion to Charismatic Christianity in Arunachal Pradesh.

The 95% of the 27 respondents agreed that they speak in tongues through the anointing work of the Holy Spirit, at any time, any place. However, most of those respondents agreed that on Sunday worship services more members tend to speak in tongues. One Christian Revival Church pastor in Itanagar explained that, "there is no restriction of time and space to speak in tongues. Once we start worshipping God by shouting three times "praise the Lord", then some among the believers would automatically start speaking in tongues, while mass spoken prayer in the church is the main source of invoking the Holy Spirit to initiate speaking in tongues."[9]

As per their answer, to one of the questions in the questionnaire which I asked regarding the support of family members concerning speaking in tongues, 85% of the family members agreed on speaking in tongues in their family. If a mother or father speaks in tongues during a family fellowship or prayer time, the whole family would keep silent and wait eagerly, to see whether the Lord has any message for the family or for the Church. An active member of Christian Revival Church, expressed,

> Whenever I start speaking in tongues, my husband and children would silently wait. If the Lord has any message for our family, He would reveal to us through the speaking in tongues. Then followed by prophecy and after I spoke in an unknown language, I would interpret it into Assamese or Hindi, so that all of them could understand the meaning.'[10]

This is transformation of family life among church members, and certain unification among families, through speaking in tongues. It could likewise be delineated and understood that the theological significance of the Holy Spirit is experienced through ordinary people's worship of God by fully immersing themselves in the heart of God, which Jesus promised in the book of John and fulfilled in Acts of the Apostles. As Frank D. Macchia rightly notes, speaking in tongues is further confirmation of the 'Sanctified Ones' on the baptism of the Spirit and 'the sanctification of human speech.'[11] In the context of Christian Revival Church one can also determine the baptism of the Spirit in the church or family through speaking in tongues. Anderson identifies that Pentecostal-Charismatic Christianity was made globally known because of the charisma of speaking in tongues.[12] Indeed, it is the eruption of speaking in tongues that caused a zeal among many mainline churches that also wanted to experience this charisma.[13] Such a zeal for experience, even among the most ordinary believers in the remotest area of Arunachal Pradesh, appears to have been fulfilled through the power of the Holy Spirit. It has been said that in almost every family of the Christian Revival Church members seeks the confirmation of the spirit baptism through speaking in tongues.

Although the healing of sick people is one of the key impacts of conversion to CRC, the intuition of speaking in tongues in the process of conversion is very much recommended by most of the believers in the church. They believe that it is through speaking in tongues that the true messages of the church, of love and unity, are revealed and spread through society. A senior evangelist of Arunachal Pradesh Christian Revival Church Council, expressed that, "our every programme and plan, be it for a family, the Church and social concern activities, we depend on the vision, prophecy and the speaking in tongues. Without these, we have no power of movement."[14] The senior evangelist's statement links to what McGee argues: "[f]rom this vantage, to be Pentecostal meant that one prayed in tongues, an experiential dynamic from which one derived spiritual power."[15] According to some elderly believers of CRC, a church without prophecy, vision and speaking in tongues is a 'dry driven' church in the 21st century, where everything is required to be proven using evidence and miracles of God. They claimed that the vibrant spiritual activities in the church constitute the practical experience of God's presence in the worship services and socially concerned ministries. Cartledge's finding of empirical theology, reflects a parallel experience with what CRC adherents claim to experience daily in their praxis with God in the Spirit.[16]

Role of Individual Practical Life

The primary intention of the five testimonial type of questions as mentioned above was to classify how far respondents' conversion to Charismatic Christianity were linked to the stage models of conversion; and how they contributed to practical and social life, cultural transformation, and whether they had benefited socio-economic growth? I have incorporated Rambo's seven stage models of analysing and interpreting the conversion process of each potential religious convert to Christianity, which was augmented by Gooren's model of religious affiliation, disaffiliation, and re-affiliation. In this section, Goorens' delineation of related social conversion appears to have corresponded to the context of Arunachal Pradesh. I intend to relate Snow and Machalek's finding of *the convert as a social type,* which I see as the original source Gooren used in his studies on conversion. Under the seven stage models of the conversion process, an encounter with God appears to have had much impact on the personal and family life of the converts in Arunachal Pradesh. As one pastor expressed:

> Yes, I often felt of encounter with God followed by my conversion. My first encounter with God was a dream that God called me by showing Joel 2:12-13, and Isaiah 6:8-9. I felt a complete change in me after seeing such dreams, and after that, I followed God with my regular prayer and fasting. Now at present, in my every prayer hour, I see vision and revelation while I am in my personal ministry of healing and deliverance.[17]

Joram Dol's encounter with God can be linked to the commitment stage of conversion as we can see that he states that he then followed "God with my regular prayer and fasting", which exhibits a sense of loyalty to God after his conversion event. Another respondent stated that; "making any sort of commitment to God and his church is not an easy matter. One should think more than twice to have a commitment to God; because the failure of commitment with God can bid a curse upon our family and even to the society where we live."[18] Another respondent, answering the fourth and sixth questions (on ritual commitment) said that, "actually, no, I don't have any commitment to God, but I just made a simple way of the fact that believing God is to follow him till the end of my life journey. If Baptism is a kind of ritual commitment, then I have done it. Or if prayer and fasting can be considered as a ritual commitment, I do them as often as I can. Other than these, I have no other certain commitment to God."[19]

One way or another I have integrated the perspectives of Peter Chetri in relation to the consequences stage, as it clearly concerns the significance of consequences in Rambo's conversion stage model. As per my critical observation through structured and semi-structured questionnaires, interactions and interviews, it can be seen that it is a point of crisis that has the main impact on the conversion process. Encounters with God in various ways, and overcoming crises in the family and society after conversion experience event, has a significant aspect of true-life source for their Christian faith and journey till date. Tap Taluk expressed that, "yes, through a crisis in life, while following Jesus, I have been made stronger in my faith in Christ Jesus. After conversion to Christianity, I realised, through a crisis, to depend upon Christ Jesus and my faith becomes stronger, thereby having my faith journey successfully till date." Crisis, as interpreted by Rambo, is the turning point for the potential convert. According to the fifth testimonial questioned answers, they too identified and have thought that the crisis is the turning point of their faith, followed by conversion. The quest and interaction have quite complexities in relation to the Christian experiences in the context though my first in the six set questions was asked in relation to the quest and interaction, but none of them could answer what exactly is the religious quest or search. However, one of the five respondents have suggested that after knowing other major religion's forms of worship and teachings, he identified Christianity as the best religion in the world, a faith in which the truth is revealed in the religious scripture.

Along with the questionnaire and questions, I also met some elite members of the Nyishi people who are from mainline Churches around Itanagar. I carried out some significant informal interactions and discussions with these people about the Christian concern for the social-religious and socio-economic development of the community, which are briefly explained.

As far as conversion to Christianity is concerned, it has often been observed that conversion causes a change in people's character and behaviour, which automatically affects the society. For example, family and individual lifestyles have been transformed in a fuller means of life. In evaluations of the five persons' answers to the six questions, after conversion to Christianity (and not only to Charismatic Christianity), one should by any means start to observe some changes to the family and community life, without which changing of religion has no meaning at all. As Peter Chetri expresses that:

Social transformation means something that we do among men to human races. Social change is a vital part of Christian ministry, as fourth Ten Commandment commands between God and men, and the sixth Ten Commandments between the men to men. Following Jesus should result in us a social transformation, and our lives should influence the society. The disciples of Jesus turned the world upside down; Martin Luther by following Jesus brought a great social reform. Therefore, it is by following Jesus; the outcome will be great, and this should be our ministry.[20]

I have attempted to recapitulate the conversion experiences and the faith journeys of these five testimonial interviewees. They have unanimously suggested and their thoughtful and meaningful answers have helped my findings in this field. Their answers clearly acknowledge that conversion to Christianity results in a true change of both the individual and family life, followed by social transformation, due to a commitment to follow God in one's life, whatever the consequences may be.

Role of Divine Healing

Divine healing, as briefly highlighted above is one of the most incorporated churches' dynamic basis of conversion to Christian church in the region where this study is focused. It is practically undeniably believed and testified by the adherents; a church without divine healing aspect would be a church without recipient of liberating spirit from God. One of the most stimulating impact of divine healing in the church is that it not only manifests the physical and spiritual well-being of the devotees, but it also has ignited the spirit of unity among Christianity in particular and social arena in general. It rightly relates the words of D. D. Smith, "all denominations are here for the purpose of showing forth that Christ is the perfect redeemer – He first unifies man by making him whole, proving that He is the Redeemer of the soul and the body, and then brings us together in that close union with Christ which brings us closer to each other."[21]

As has been highlighted, divine healing as an integral part of churches' major impact of the conversion or drawing people to Christ, the attention has been made to collect data from some churches' experiencing of the particular factor leading to massive impact on conversion/change. For this I have formulated a method of questionnaire focusing on the divine healing aspect and have gathered the testimonial evidences from different churches around the capital vicinity (Itanagar-Naharlagun, AP).

Glancing into the data collection through questionnaire, I distributed 100 questions to the four different major denominational churches around the aforementioned area, namely; Baptist, Catholic, Revival, Pentecostal, however, collected 40 questions answer from Baptist church. It is enormously unbelievable, as out of 100 questionnaire papers, the 99% agreed to have believed in the healing power of Christian Church through prayer in the name of Jesus Christ. Out of 100 answers, 60 have agreed to be permanently healed from their sickness, 40 have reported to be re-felt from their sickness after healing through prayers following some years, and 10 have spent to the other treatments, for example, medical, other faith, and local medication.

The above brief report and analysis on divine healing impact of conversion to Christianity altogether proves that the majority of Christians in Arunachal Pradesh have undeniably become Christian or de-affiliated from other faith to affiliate into the Christian church is certainly very specific reasons, as exemplified in the healing aspect.

Integration of mainline Church and Christian Revival Church

The study on congregation was complemented by the opportunity to meet other church leaders and believers during the Christmas and New Year celebrations in December 2015. The chance to meeting and interact with these church leaders and members, added depth to the research, and gave significant additional information about the growth and development of Christianity in general in Arunachal Pradesh.

As mentioned the denominational misunderstanding within Christianity in the region until recent years was disintegration. However, there has been a progression in regard to unity and understanding between the Charismatic and the mainline churches in the state, in comparison to the recent past. One significant development is the establishment of prayer tower or centres by mainline churches, for example, the Baptists. Until recently, the system and practice of prayer towers/houses were mainly the maintained by the Pentecostal-Charismatic Christian churches.[22] The mainline churches usually practiced worshipping God in the well-established church buildings rather than in more temporary prayer buildings.[23] However, the establishment of prayer towers or centres among the mainline churches is a very significant sign of a more unified Christian mission in the region, although some competitive attitude towards one another may still be prevalent.

The views expressed by Baptist Church leaders and members were highly appreciable of this development. As one prominent Baptist Church leader states:

> We obliviously quarrelled and fought within the Christianity; criticising one another until recent years. But, once I opened John chapter seventeen, the modelled prayer of Jesus Christ and meditated on that passage for some

days. I was so inspired by the Spirit of God, how vital and important it is to unite and work together for all Christians for the extension of God's kingdom on this earth before Jesus Christ returns to judge the world.[24]

Similar narratives have been expressed by leaders and believers of my local mission Office, appreciating Christian Revival Church and other Charismatic churches for their model example of spiritual growth in the region through their method of establishing Prayer Towers or Centres, which have become the sources of spiritual power for all Christians in Arunachal Pradesh. Today, it is possible to see many people flocking around the Prayer Towers, seeking God's guidance for their individual and family matters.[25] Until recent years, the three-time exclamatory, Praise the Lord, during Church worship service was practised only in the Pentecostal-Charismatic Churches, but this practice of praising and shouting the name of the Lord today can be commonly heard in most of the Christian churches in the region. "We must by all means unite and work together if at all, we Christians believe that Arunachal is for Christ, as the saying goes, "united we stand divided, we fall."[26] The positivity of the Charismatic churches, and not only the Christian Revival Christian, are very much applauded by many elderly and educated Christians. Nevertheless, as already identified in the section on methodology, the market metaphors of Pentecostal-Charismatic Christianity - as a competitive way of doing God's mission - apparently still exists. The same attitude is still overtly or covertly evident within Christendom, as followers practice denominational revival crusades, seminars, and mass involvements.

We see these days in Arunachal Pradesh, crusade after crusades; Revival Church crusade, Pentecostal Church crusades, Assemblies of God Church crusades, Baptist Church Crusades, and even the Catholic Churches have started organising spiritual awakening programmes. Christianity in our place is becoming like the competitors of crusades, uttered by an elderly man.[27]

Doctrinal Confusion - the Twofold Baptism

Upon the brief reflection of a valued incorporated Charismatic and mainline church concerning the significant of unity, I carried out a brief survey apropos the issues of water and spirit baptism within the Christian Revival Church in the region.[28] The confidentiality of such doctrinal and sacramental contradiction within the Charismatic movement appeared to have cunningly shyness. I approached certain members of the denomination, seeking their thoughts and understanding in relation to the issues. Most candidates stated that they act upon things according to the guidance and inspiration of the Holy Spirit. Making such statements as per scholarly observation and analysis is imprecise in regard to doctrinal and sacramental reliability and necessary of rectifying the issues in the context. According to the doctrine of biblical baptism, the issue seems to be a main aspect of confusion in the regional Charismatic movement, a situation that stirs me to briefly explore on this issue.[29]

Significant reliable and practical sources relating to these issues have instead been made known by other denomination members who used to attend and participate several times in the so-called spiritual retreat programmes in one of the Prayer Centres of Christian Revival Church. For example, a woman, one of the counsellors in the Nyishi Baptist Church Council's prayer centre, explained that "the practice of second water baptism in the Christian Revival Church depends upon the strong and weakness of an individual who attends to their Prayer Centres for fasting and prayer, seeking some spiritual guidance and help."[30]

The above brief experiment stimulated me to delve into some of the differences between Spirit and water baptisms, differences that may potentially have been a point of confusion in the Christian Revival Church progress in the state. Precisely, the knowledge of the history of Christianity through the ages has undeniably been fragmented, both in the biblical and theological concept of the twofold baptism, which obstructed Christianity within and without. This obstruction has consistently made confusion to the authenticity of a sound doctrine of baptism even in far-flung places such as Arunachal Pradesh.

Linking to the context of Arunachal Pradesh and the issues of baptism, it is important to briefly delineate the biblical aspects of baptism. Undoubtedly, when one discusses the twofold baptism, it is a prerequisite to ensure the books of Luke and Acts for a clear meaning of the term 'baptism', of both water and Spirit. However, I do not intend to have a lengthy discussion here regarding the ongoing debates and arguments among the different denominations within Christianity on the twofold baptism, but instead offer a brief elucidation. For the sake of brevity, I propose primarily to infer the views of Sarah Hinlicky Wilson, who aligns her discussion with James Dunn's understanding of the twofold baptism, while looking into the accounts of Luke and Acts.[31] While critically assessing Dunn's and other contemporary New Testament scholars' delineation of baptism, Wilson clarifies that the New Testament understanding of the twofold baptism is conventionally coherent when we turn to the accounts of Luke and Acts. As Wilson states, "Luke's primary purpose is to distinguish John's water baptism without the Spirit from Christian water baptism with the Spirit."[32] Returning to the context of the Charismatic Church movement in Arunachal Pradesh, one can argue that the level of understanding of water baptism still parallels the idea of John's water baptism without the spirit.[33] In Christian Revival Church practice, according to my careful observations, they have an uncertainty of water baptism in other denomination. Their uncertainty is based on what Macchia identifies as the question of whether the Spirit is bestowed at baptism, in confirmation, or in the complex of sacraments of initiation.[34] This is slightly analogous to the question regarding the practice of infant baptism from the non-infant practice churches. Or in other words, Christian Revival Church doubts that water baptism in other denominations is initiating the Spirit. In contrast, Karl Barth systematises that the Holy Spirit is already at work once a faithless person comes to the faithful God through the inspiration of the words of God when it is preached.[35] In obedience to the command and call of God, the water baptism is actually performed by the power of the Holy Spirit.[36] In practice, there may be a few adherents in every Christian denomination who could have taken water baptism without the work and inspiration of the Spirit. Nevertheless, in contexts such as Arunachal Pradesh, where Christianity is still new, most of the members are believed to have been baptised with water after a clear conviction of faith in Christ Jesus. It is arguable that Barth's comments are absolutely authentic in the context of Arunachal Pradesh Christianity as a whole, and that the baptism of water is believed to be performed with the initiation of the Spirit, as Wilson identifies after reflecting on the books of Luke and Acts as have been mentioned above.

Endnotes

[1] Nunthara, C. 'Social Change in North-East India: A Christian Perspective' in *Society and Culture in North-East India: A Christian Perspective* (ed. Saral K. Chatterji), 1996, ISPCK, Delhi, 100.

[2] Nelson, Douglas J. 1981, *For such a time as this: The Story of Bishop J. Seymour and the Azusa Street, a search for Pentecostal/Charismatic roots* (PhD Thesis), Birmingham: University of Birmingham, 14.

[3] McGee, Gary B. ' "Latter Rain" Falling in the East: Early-Twentieth-Century Pentecostalism in India and the Debate over Speaking in Tongues', *American Theological Library Association* (September 1999), 651-52.

[4] I interacted with him on 13th December 2016 after the Sunday Worship Service.

[5] Nyokter Abom is an active believer of CRC, Itanagar. I interacted with her on the 29th December 2015 in an informal discussion at her home.

[6] Macchia, Frank D. 2006, *Baptized in the Spirit: A Global Pentecostal Theology*, Michigan: Grand Rapid, 83.

[7] Anderson, *To the Ends of the Earth*, 8.

[8] Anderson, *To the Ends of the Earth*, 8.

[9] I interviewed him on the 2nd January 2016 at a Baptist Church fellowship meeting.

[10] McGee, "Latter Rain", 651.

[11] See empirical theology, page 12.

[12] The quotation one which I have inserted is the answer given in written form by Joram Dol to the second question of the sixth questions on the stage of encounter after conversion.

[13] I met this person and interacted with him on 4th January 2016 at his home.

[14] The fourth sixth of the testimonial question was asked to relate the commitment stage model of Rambo's seven stage models of conversion.

[15] He is a Youth Director of Christian Revival Church, Itanagar. The quotation is a direct quote from the answer he wrote for the sixth question, with a slight correction to the English.

[16] Heather D. Curtis, 2011. 'The Global Character of Nineteen-Century Divine Healing' in *Pentecostal and Charismatic Healing*, (Edited) Brown, G. Candy, Oxford Press, 49.

[17] A Prayer Tower or Centre is a place other than community Church where people worship God for longer hours or days, often with fasting. People set out one week to one month for praying and fasting in the prayer tower or centre.

[18] Presently, there are at least five Prayer Centres of Nyishi Baptist Church Council in Arunachal Pradesh, and one Prayer Tower of Apatani Baptist Association.

[19] The one whom I interacted was one of the leaders in Apatani Baptist Association. This is the youngest Christian Association in Arunachal Pradesh, India.

[20] On 31st December 2015, my family and I visited a Baptist Prayer Centre to give thanks to God. In the Prayer Centre we saw a lot of people flocking to give thanks to God for their success that year.

[21] The respondent is one of the principal staff of a Bible College in the region.

[22] On 16th December 2015, over a cup of coffee at a local restaurant, I had a discussion with this man, who is from a Baptist church and does not want his name to be mentioned here.

[23] The issue of second time water baptism system in the CRC movement is identified as doctrinally contrary to the biblical basis of baptism.

[24] The researcher's observation on similar issues faced formerly has been reprimanded as it reflects in this research studies.

[25] Mrs Yukar Yapaq is one of the Counsellors in the Nyishi Baptist Church Council's Prayer Centre, who often goes to the CRC Prayer Centres for spiritual retreat. I interviewed with her on the 21st December 2016 at NBCC Prayer Centre, Naharlagun, and Arunachal Pradesh, India. As per Yapaq's observation, the enforcement of second water baptism is fully depends upon the critical condition of an individual where compulsion is unavoidable.

[26] Wilson, Hinlicky, S. 'Water Baptism and Spirit Baptism in Luke-Acts – Another Reading of the Evidence', PNEUMA 38 (2016) 476–501. See also James Dunn and his (in) famous work *Baptism in the Holy Spirit: A Re-Examination of the New Testament Teaching on the Gift of the Spirit in Relation to Pentecostalism Today*, 2nded. (London: scm, 2010).

[27] Wilson, Hinlicky, S. "Water Baptism and Spirit Baptism", *PNEUMA*, 38. 501.

[28] As far as other Christians' testimonies are concerned, the Christian Revival Church in Arunachal Pradesh seemed not believing the other Churches' water baptism as the combined baptism of the Holy Spirit.

[29] Macchia, *Baptism in the Spirit*. 72.

[30] Barth, Karl, 1969. *Church Dogmatics, - The Doctrine of Reconciliation* (Volume IV), Edinburgh: T & T. Clark, 35-40. In this commentary, Barth places the baptism of Spirit in the first place and the baptism of water in the second, which indicates that the Spirit is at work among believers even before water baptism

[31] Barth, 40.

Conclusion

Identifying the locus of Charismatic Church and its diverse movements in Arunachal Pradesh has been an intriguing area. However, it has been somewhat complex for the researcher to appropriately incorporate the context and practices of the region with the work of scholars of conversion. For example, understanding and reading about conversion to Christianity in general and conversion to Charismatic Church in particular, and relating this with the seven stage models. The principal cause of this challenge is primarily due to the insufficiency of study resources on such issues, for instance, the shaky like nature of Charismatic church movements in the region. However, an attempt has been made to comprehensively and critically analyse the significant areas of the growth and development of Christianity in general, and the Charismatic Church in particular. The practical theology of peoples' experience with God through daily spiritual activities, such as healing and speaking in tongues in the Church is some intriguing areas of discovery. It can certainly be seen that conversion to Charismatic Christianity has had a positive and transformational impact on society, community, while identifying that most of the seven stage models of conversion are applicable to the conversion process and conversion events, both charismatically and evangelically, however, though the potential converts failed to be aware of the fact. However, from my structured questionnaires, questions and interviews, it can undeniably be argued that the cases of conversion process, events and experiences are certainly useful in the context of transition in the religious journey.

Although it has not been possible to comprehensively join the practices of the Charismatic Church in Arunachal Pradesh with the arguments of scholars of religious conversion, however, the authenticity of the true meaning and significance of Christian conversion has been adopted into a wider understanding of interpreting the meaning and in-depth awareness of conversion in connection to the context have been made possible.

From the findings and analysis of questionnaires, questions and interviews with various church leaders, believers, and the focused congregation, it is indisputably identified that there is some theological and pneumatological confusion within the Charismatic movements in the region, among the followers and leaders merely interpreting phenomena and practice as the move of God in the Spirit. The lack of proper knowledge about pneumatology, as expressed in the answers to the first question of the sixth testimonial questions could potentially be due to the absence of theological training and reading literatures by adherents. The lack of accessibility to theological books and articles in the region, and in these churches, hinder this theological development. Nevertheless, the evidence of social transformation in both the smaller or bigger areas of the society has inseparably been impact out of the conversion experiences in the lives of converts. Social impact could have been the results of the converts' believing in the power and work of the Holy Spirit in various ways. The simplicity of theology and pneumatology is very much affected by the practicality of the ordinary means of praise and adoration to God. This is mainly displayed by the expression of mass spoken prayer, constant prayer and fasting by the majority believers of the Charismatic Christianity, together leading the way to spiritual renewal movements, which has in turn inspired the mainline churches to grasp this spirituality as important aspects of their own church growth.

Bibliography

Anderson, A. H., 2013. *To the Ends of the Earth: Pentecostalism and the Transformation of World Christianity,* Oxford: Oxford University Press.

Barth, K., 1969. *Church Dogmatics, the Doctrine of Reconciliation* (Volume IV), Edinburgh: T & T. Clark.

Bernard, R. H., 1994. *Research methods in anthropology: qualitative and quantitative approaches,* second edition, Walnut Creek, CA: Alta Mira Press.

Bergunder, M., 2008. *The South Indian Pentecostal Movement in the Twentieth Century,* Grand Rapids, Michigan: William B. Eerdmans Publishing Company.

Bhagabati, C. A., 2004. 'Indigenous Faiths and Customs: Some Observations.' In: M. C. Behera and C. K. Sarit, ed. *Indigenous Faith and Practices of the Tribes of Arunachal Pradesh.* Itanagar: Himalayan Publishers.

Borang, G., 2013. *Changing Social and Cultural Institutions of Adi (Padam) of Arunachal Pradesh,* Itanagar: Himalayan Publishers and Distributors.

Borang, K., 2004. Philosophy of Donyi-Polo, In: M. Tamo and C. K. Sarit, ed. *Understanding Tribal Religion,* New Delhi: Mittal Publications, pp.40-42.

Bryant, D. M., 1999. 'Conversion in Christianity: from without and within,' In: Lamb Christopher A. and M. Darrol Bryant, ed. *Religious Conversion: Contemporary Practices and Controversy,* New York: CASSELL p.178.

Burgess, S. M., 1994. 'Cutting the Taproot: The Modern Pentecostal Movement and its Traditions,' In: Christopher Thomas, Rick D. Moore and Steven J. Land, ed. *Spirit and Renewal: Essays in Honour of J. Rodman Williams,* Sheffield: Sheffield Academic Press, pp.60-61.

Cartledge, M. J., 2003. *Practical Theology: Charismatic and Empirical Perspectives,* Cumbria: Paternoster Press.

Cartledge, M. J., 2013. 'Testimony of the Spirit: Rescripting Ordinary Pentecostal Theology.' In: E-Book. *Explorations in Practical Pastoral and Empirical Theology,* Oxford: ASHGATE, p.14.

Cartledge, M. J., 2006. *Encountering the Spirit: Charismatic Tradition*, London: Longman and Todd Ltd.

Cartledge, M. J., 2010. *Testimony of the Spirit: Rescripting Ordinary Pentecostal Theology*, Burlington: ASGATE.

Chan, S., 2000. *Pentecostal Theology and the Christian Spiritual Tradition*, Sheffield: Sheffield Academic Press.

Conn, W., 1986. *Christian Conversion: A Developmental Interpretation of Autonomy and Surrender*, New Jersey: Paulist Press.

Danggen, B., 2007. *A Comparative Study of Bon Religion of Ancient Tibet with Donyi-Polo Faith of the Adis of Arunachal Pradesh*, Itanagar: Preety Publishers and Distributors.

Davi, T., 2004. 'Relevance of Tribal Religion: An Overview.' In: Tamo, Mibang and Sarit, Chaudhuri, ed. *Understanding Tribal Religion*, New Delhi: Mittal Publications, pp.9-10.

Dawar, J. L., 'Religious Conversion and Contending Responses', *Understanding Tribal Religion*, (Ed. Tamo, Mibang & Sarit, Chaudhuri K.), New Delhi: Mittal Publications, 161-2.

Drema, T., 'Sacred Places of Monpas of Arunachal Pradesh' In: Tamo Mibang and Sarit K. Chaudhuri, (ed). *Understanding Tribal Religion*, New Delhi: Mittal Publications, p.210.

Fowler, J. 1999., 'Practical Theology and Social Sciences' in: Friedrich Schweitzer, Johannes A. Van der Ven, (ed.) *International Perspectives*, New York: Peter Lang, 291-292.

Gooren, H., 2010. *Religious Conversion and Disaffiliation: Tracing Patterns of Change in Faith Practices*, New York: Palgrave Macmillan.

Jevons, B. F., 1908. 'Hellenism and Christianity' *the Harvard Theological Review*, 1(2), 69-188.

Lamb, A., 1964. *The China-India Border: The Origins of the Disputed Boundaries*, Oxford: Oxford University Press.

Martin, B., 2006. 'Pentecostal Conversion and the limits of the market metaphor' in: *Peer Review Journal* (Vol.35). Leiden: Brill, 61-91.

Michael, L. J., 1971. The Shape of Religious Instruction: A Social Science Approach, Indiana: Religious Education Press INC.

Milton, G., 2013. 'Understanding Pentecostal Conversion: an Empirical Study.' (PhD thesis) University: Birmingham.

O'Dea, T. F., 1966. *The Sociology of Religion*, New Jersey: Prentice Hall.

O'Dea, T. F., 1966. *Foundations of Modern Sociology Series: The Sociology of Religion*, New Jersey: Prentice Hall.

Omengyo, C. N. 2011., 'New Wine in an Old Wine Bottle: Charismatic Healing in the Mainline Churches in Ghana' in: Brown, Candy Gunther, ed. *Global Pentecostal and Charismatic Healing*, New York: Oxford University Press, 236-7. 2012. *Oxford Dictionary of English*, Oxford: University Press.

Pandey, D., 2006. *History of Arunachal Pradesh: earliest time to 1972 A.D*, Pasighat: Bani Mandir Publication.

Rambo, L. R., 1993. *Understanding Religious Conversion*, Michigan: Grand Rapids.

Rikbo, T., 1998. 'Donyi-Polo Faith and Practice of the Adis' In: Behera, M. C. and, S. K Chaudhuri, ed. *Indigenous Faith and Practices of the Tribes of Arunachal Pradesh*, Itanagar: Himalaya Publishers, pp.57-59.

Orsi, R., 1997. 'Everyday Miracles: The Study of Lived Religion.' In: David D. Hall, ed. *Lived Religion in America: toward a History of Practice*, New Jersey: Princeton University Press, p.8.

Smith, G. R., 2011. The Church Militant: A Study of "Spiritual Warfare". (The Anglican Charismatic Renewal) PhD Thesis, University: Birmingham.

Thomas, J., 2010. Church and the Formation of Naga Political Identity, 1918-1997, PhD Thesis, Centre for Historical Studies, Jawaharlal Nehru University.

Journals

Boughton, J.M., 2002. 'The Bretton Woods proposal: a brief look' in: *Political Science Quarterly), 42.6, (JSTOR), 564-76. Cox, C. 2002, 'What health care assistants know about clean hands' Nursing Times*, (Spring Issue), pp.647-85.

Brown, C. G., 2011. 'Global Pentecostal and Charismatic Healing' *Oxford Scholarship Online*, (Oxford University Press), 4-5.

Corrie, J. 2015. Theological Education in Latin America: Bolivia as a Case Study. *Transformation*, 32.4, (Pneuma), 281-293.

Eriksen, A., 2014. Sarah's Sinfulness Egalitarianism: Denied Difference, and Gender in Pentecostal Christianity. *The Anthropology of Christianity*, (University of Chicago Press Journal), 262-270.

Klaver, and Miranda 2011. 'Embodied Temporalities in Global Pentecostal Conversion' (Ethnos Publications, 76), 421-425.

Gooren, H., 2006. 'The Religious Market Model and Conversion: Towards a New Approach' *Exchange*, 35 (1) (Ecclesiastical Law Journal), 39-60.

Halama, P., 2015. 'Empirical Approach to Typology of Religious Conversion' *Pastoral Psychology*, 64 (Springer), 187-194.

Kawulich, B. B., 2005. 'Participant Observation as a Data Collection Method' *Qualitative Social Research*, 6 (2) (Art. 43), 466-475.

Haynes, N., 2014. 'Affordances and Audiences: Finding the Difference Christianity Makes' in: *Current Anthropology*, 55 (Peer Reviewed Journal), 358-365.

Hayward, D. R. and N. Krause, 2015. 'Aging, Social Developmental and Cultural Factors in Changing Patterns of Religious Involvement over a 32-Year Period: An Age Cohort Analysis of 80 Countries. *Journal of Cross-Cultural Psychology*, 46 (Sage Publications.), 979-995.

Kirkland, W. 'Spirituality versus Spiritism: A Confession of Faith' in: *The North American Review*, 213(JSTOR), 1921, 83-85.

Longo, & Kim-Spoon, 2014. 'What Drives Apostates and Converters? The Social and Familial Antecedents of Religious Change among Adolescents' in: *Psychology of Religion and Spirituality*, 6.4 (PubMed Central Journal), 284-291.

Lunn, J., 2009. 'Paying Attention: The Task of Attending in Spiritual Direction and Practical Theology' in: *Journal of Practical Theology* 2, (Taylor & Francis Online), 19-32.

Lyall, D., 2009. 'So, what is Practical Theology?' in: *Journal of Practical Theology*, 2 (Taylor & Francis Online), 317-325.

Martin, B., 2006. 'Pentecostal Conversion and the Limits of the Market Metaphor' in: *Exchange*, 35(BRILL), 61-91.

Marlett, J. D., 1997. 'Conversion Methodology and the Case of Cardinal Newman' in: *Theological Studies*, 58 (BRILL), 61-91.

Max, B., 2014. 'A Competition for Converts in Arunachal Pradesh' in: *India ink*, 21(New York Times), 2.

Naidoo, M. 2015. 'Ministerial Formation and Practical Theology in South Africa' in: *International Journal of Practical Theology*, 19 (Research Gate), pp.166-178.

Robbins, J., 2004. 'The Globalization of Pentecostal and Charismatic Christianity' in: *Annual Review of Anthropology*, 33 (JSTOR), 119-127.

Kahn, P. J., A. L. Greene, 2004. "Seeing Conversion Whole": Testing a Model of Religious Conversion. *Pastoral Psychology*, 52(3), 233-258.

Richardson, J. T., 1985. Active versus Passive Convert: Paradigm in Conflict Conversion Recruitment research. *Journal for the Scientific Study of Religion*, 24(2), 165-178.

Saunders, G. R., 1995. "The Crisis of Presence in Italian Pentecostal conversion." *American Ethnologist*, 324-340.

Schilderman, H., 2014. 'Religion as Concept and Measure' in: Journal of Empirical Theology, 27(Radboud University), 1-16.

Schwab, H. L., 1910. 'Is Christianity a Moral Code a Religion?' *The Harvard Theological Review*, 3(3) (JSTOR), 271-297.

Snow, D. A., R. Machalek, 1993. 'The Convert as Social Type; Sociological Theory' 1 *Phil Papers*, pp.259-282.

Starbuck, D. E., 1897. 'A Study of Conversion' the American Journal of Psychology. *JSTOR*, 268-308.

Swatos, Williams H. Kivisto, Peter. 1991. 'Max Weber as "Christian Sociologist"' *Journal for the Scientific Study of Religion*, 30 (4) (Willey), 564-570.

Wilson, H. S., 2016. Water Baptism and Spirit Baptism in Luke-Acts – Another Reading of the Evidence, 38 (PNEUMA), pp. 476-501.

Magazines/Newspaper

Bomjen, J., 2014. *Souvenir CRC-ESS Sector, Itanagar*, Itanagar: Amar Bajwa.

Eastern Sky Media, Itanagar, Arunachal Pradesh http://easternskymedia.co.in/tag/town-baptist-church

Dodum, S., 2012. *Souvenir: APCRCC Silver Jubilee (1987 – 2012)*, Naharlagun, Eureka Offset & Imaging Systems.

Fernando, F. 2014. 'Ministry in Nagaland' *Revival Magazine: A Spiritual Alive Perspective on Christian Living*, http://revivalmag.com/article/ministry-nagaland.

Liankhankhup, S. 2015. 'A Study of Hindu and Christian Mission in Arunachal Pradesh' in: *www.facebook.com/notes/* liankhankhup sektak.